Simon Hattenstone

Simon Hattenstone was born in 1962 and is the Film Editor and a writer at the *Guardian*. He is the father of two children and lives with the journalist Diane Taylor. *Out Of It* is his first book.

SCEPTRE

Out Of It

SIMON HATTENSTONE

SCEPTRE

First published in 1998 by Hodder and Stoughton
First published in paperback in 1999 by Hodder and Stoughton
A division of Hodder Headline PLC
A Sceptre Paperback

10 9 8 7 6 5 4 3 2 1

All characters in this publication are fictitious and any resemblance to real persons, living or dead, is purely coincidental.

A CIP catalogue record for this book is available from the British Library

ISBN 0 340 71869 2

Typeset by Palimpsest Book Production Limited,
Polmont, Stirlingshire
Printed and bound in Great Britain by
Clays Ltd, St Ives PLC, Bungay, Suffolk

Hodder and Stoughton
A division of Hodder Headline PLC
338 Euston Road
London NW1 3BH

To Mum

Prologue

It was about fifteen years afterwards that I first noticed it. Well, had my attention drawn to it. There was a woman at work, big, Argentinian, voluptuous, could have been snatched from one of those magic-realist novels. I called her Evita. She said she could read my future and took my hand in hers and fixed the trellises in the sun. It was a loud, pissy, happy summer's day, a Friday, and there were empty beer bottles lined up on her desk like a firing squad. The various conversations – three or four of them, swirling around the one desk – seemed to stop. I asked if I was going to be chopped down on a Zebra on the way home and laughed a sceptic's laugh. She tried to sound casual, but Evita was never a great pretender. 'No, no, no. You will live a long time, past eighty I think. See here, your line goes long and straight and powerful, and then you waver, you have a serious illness, later on, but you pull through, and you go on long and straight and powerful for years afterwards.' 'That will be the cancer,' I said trying to balance my cigarette butt on top of one of the bottles. Evita was still holding my hand. 'So what's the problem?'

'I've never seen this.' Our hands were becoming sticky, and she scraped her nail along my ticklish lifeline. 'Your lifeline is straight and strong but look back, further, further, right back to near the beginning, your childhood. Your line just leaves you and starts again. It fades out, slowly, slowly and then just dies and starts again. You have two lives.'

Chapter One

The breakfast show was on Radio 1 in the hall. Little Jimmy Osmond was singing 'I'll be your long-haired lover from Liverpool and I'll do anything you say.' I couldn't work out if I was envious of him or sorry for him. So ridiculous in that fat, white suit – an embryonic Elvis squealing like a stuck pig through those presidential teeth. He was only nine, I think. My age. More or less my weight. I was a bit of a porker, too. Nine years old, almost nine stone. Sometimes I wondered if you put on a stone for every year, but I knew that my grandma with the stick and commode wasn't seventy-seven stone.

I felt strange. I was trying to sing along to little Jimmy, and every time I got to Liverpool my teeth started trilling on the L. It was cold but not that cold. Dad was getting the car out, and it was a dark November morning, and I was shivering for Utah. My mouth was dry, my throat sore and my tongue was flicking snake-like at my palette to scratch away the itch. Underneath my blazer my shirt was moist, my tummy was wet, my belly button full of water. Mum spoke to me in an echo. My head was heavy. I'd never even thought of my head having a weight before, it was just there above my shoulders. Mum was speaking, and I couldn't hear. A wall of steel had dropped between my ears and my eyes. There was drilling and white flashes. My head had turned into a building site.

I crawled upstairs, slid into my warmest pyjamas, closed the curtains, shut my eyes and tried to distract myself from my head, the pain. If my hair grew an inch every four weeks, how long would it take me to become Marc Bolan? I couldn't work it out. If my parents were killed in an accident who would I rather be adopted by – David Cassidy's mother in the Partridge Family, or his sister? I squeezed my eyes shut. And the white light just got brighter.

I didn't have much time for illness, didn't understand its protocol. Flu tended to be dismissed as a bit of a cold and an early night with lemon tea. I sensed my building-site head was more serious, that I'd probably be in bed for a couple of days. I hated the thought of missing two days' school, the lessons, the friends, every hour learning something new to take home.

Weeks passed. My temperature rose and rose and stabilised at around 104. My bedclothes were sodden, I was sodden, my fringe wept into my eyes. The lights were out, the curtain still drawn, the flowers on the curtains were malicious woodpeckers, not flowers any more. And when the wind blew against the open window, they fluttered and flapped and haunted me.

No one knew what was wrong. The doctor had been

around. The doctor. He was my dad's best friend, his China. Uncle Reg wasn't a real uncle, but I called him Uncle out of respect and affection. Because I'd never been ill, I associated Uncle Reg with good things – Sunday-morning visits to Dad, the smell of whisky and cigar, the football talk that was above Dad's head.

Mum would be cooking lunch and he'd always ask if it was a bad time and Dad would say no, Reg, of course it's not, can you bring in the Bells, please Marjorie, and that box of Havanas. They would sit in the lounge, and the more whisky Reg drank the jollier he became. His skin – cross-hatched with thin red contours – turned his face into a faintly exotic cheese. Dad would have one, maybe two, to keep him company and would pretend he was drinking more while Reg rumbled his way through half a bottle, talking about this and that, Manchester City, business, the girls, old Chinas, the fifties and sixties and the days down the Broughton when they were still single and my, did they know how to be single, how they were a magnet to the girls, especially you Gerald, especially you.

Reg prescribed a course of antibiotics for me. And then another. He was baffled, and Reg wasn't used to being baffled. So I think he decided it was nothing a good football match wouldn't sort out.

He told Mum there was a bug going round. But after ten days or so she became suspicious, asked her friends, and the neighbours. 'Anyone of your lot got a blinding permanent headache, violent vomiting, outrageous temperature, stiff neck, light aversion, total appetite loss, won't move out of bed, barely conscious? No, sorry, I thought not.'

Everyone loved Reg. Not only was he Dad's China, he was the Doctor, the clever one, the expert. He'd fixed every illness in Dad's family. Anything wrong, they just called out Reg, and he'd make a joke about a bunch of hypochondriacs, hand over the antibiotics form, and no need to visit again. I was letting him down, being difficult, challenging his authority. And things quickly changed. He stopped telling me the football gossip, no longer promised to take me to Maine Road to watch a match and share a cigar. He began to shout at me. He said everybody got better after two courses of antibiotics and what I needed was a good dose of fresh November air. 'You're a bleddy malingerer, Simon, that's what you are, a bleddy malingerer.'

When the fresh air didn't work and Mum said she was worried, Reg agreed to refer me to the local children's hospital. At hospital I was passed to Reg's friend Dr Barry, the consultant paediatrician.

Chapter Two

They asked crazy questions about school and my hobbies. Do you have any friends? – that was a good one. And best of all, what kind of child are you? *What kind of child am I?!!* Like you spend your days asking yourself, so Simon, what kind of child are you, *exactly*? I'd never given it a moment's thought, didn't have a clue. I knew I wasn't made for Daytime TV, I knew that much. Mum told the doctors – Barry and, I think, a psychiatrist – she wouldn't change me, that I was a pretty good son. After a while, I began to think she was making it up. Embroidering a bit. Well, if life's crap at least treat yourself to decent memories. I told the doctors she was biased, prejudiced. She'd never seen me at school, when I could be a real git.

'What, you were naughty, disobedient?' asked Dr Barry hopefully. Oh no, nothing like that I said, no, definitely not naughty. I was just unpleasant, elitist, a clever-clogs, a smarty pants, the kind of boy who would never lend so much as a felt tip or triangle to someone he didn't feel was his intellectual and social equal. Rubbish, Mum would say, her voice breaking with the betrayal. Everyone loved you, you'd do anything for anyone – even people you hardly knew. I was so proud, she said, so proud. You'd go up and down Bury Old Road on your Chopper, you were only seven when we bought it, up and down, delivering chocolates and jam and hellos for anyone, anyone! Aunts and uncles and great aunts and great uncles and agoraphobic third cousins who hadn't stepped out of the house in years, and you'd be there with your little-boy smile, and your beep of the bike, and you'd put your arm around them and say how Mum sent her love, and you'd heard so much of them, and wouldn't they please come round for tea one night.

She was snuffling, Mum was snuffling, and I was thinking, oh God isn't it bad enough without her snuffling. And he was so independent, she said, so independent, he'd go anywhere, no fear whatsoever, he didn't care if he got lost. 'You know,' she said, and gave Dr Barry a frozen stare, 'you know he loved life, every little thing. Once we were in Italy, and he got lost on the beach, the beach went on for miles. And miles. The seats were numbered one to a hundred, and then they'd start again, another one to a hundred, and again. Eight hours he was lost, the beach was deserted, we just thought he must have drowned, kids didn't get abducted in those days. And we were there in the police station waiting and waiting and hearing no news as the hours passed, and clutching each other preparing for the worst, three o'clock, four o'clock, five o'clock. I'd lost hope, and at nine o'clock he rode up on the back of a police bike, all black with sun and a tired smile on his face. And I said to the policeman, but why did no one report him, why did no one think about reporting this poor little boy walking up and down the beach, five years old, all by himself in a foreign country. And you know what he said? He said, because he didn't look worried, he didn't look upset, he pretended he was OK.'

And she stopped, and cried, and said to Dr Barry, can't you see he needs help now. And I just looked at her and thought you've got it all wrong, it's not because I was a good boy that I used to deliver the jam and presents. It was because I liked the freedom, I liked the wind at my back. The fact that other boys in my class had to ride on the pavement. And I began shouting from my bed, at Mum and at Barry and at the psychiatrist gawping at me. I started shouting, 'You never knew me, you never bloody knew me.' And I didn't know where the rage was coming from. 'I never even liked the bloody Hallé. All those times you were so proud because I went to classical music, symphonies, and all I liked was the Choc Ice in the interval, and I hated the bloody tunes. And you know what else, I would march around the playground, only a few weeks ago, finger to lips, arms stretched out, shouting Zig Heil, Zig Heil, Zig Heil. And you know why? Because I thought I was Hitler, yes Hitler, Zig Heil, Zig Heil, Zig Heil.'

When the ward doctors left, and she had calmed down, she put her hand to my head and wiped off the sweat with a tissue. You think you remember everything about yourself, you think you know everything about yourself, but you don't, she said. You were such a happy, positive little boy, and deep down you still are. Nothing's changed. Not really. When your head feels a bit better, she said, draw up two lists, one of all the things you loved before you were ill, another of all the things you hated, and see which side you come out on. *When your head feels better. When. When, bloody never.*

Pen and paper, lists, no chance. My head was imploding and she was asking me to make a shopping list. But you adapt. I didn't actually need paper and pens. With all the time – do you realise how long, just how long, twenty-four hours is when you've got nothing to do, twenty-four hours a day, sixty minutes an hour, sixty seconds a minute and each second outlasting its welcome – with all that frigging time, I was constantly formulating mental lists. The lightning and the drilling and the steel walls, the road works inside my head, jostled and jolted and distracted, but this was my new brain food, my mental press ups.

So there I am, head propped up on three pillows, stylish eye patch on right eye, (just an experiment), daylight locked out by the malicious woodpecker curtains. Hello darkness my old friend. And just to satisfy Mum and, fair do's, to pass the infinite time, I'm playing my internal *Generation Game*. Anthea does a twirl, Brucie tugs his chin, and tells me the conveyor belt of love is about to pass before my eyes and anything I can memorise I will be allowed to take home with me.

I loved school, homework, grilled steak with chips and frozen peas and mustard. Roast beef and Yorkshire pud and frozen peas and mustard. Scoobydoo. My mustard Chopper with three gears and its long black almost leather seat. I loved going on holiday to Rimini or Tenerife and getting home and Mum pulling down the tops of my trousers to show the neighbours the black line against my bottom.

Playing cricket in the garden with a tennis ball and hitting six and out over the next-door fence. Riding on the au pair's shoulders in the old days round the landing as a good-night treat and getting an erection against her neck. Taking friends to my grandparents and Grandad Noah following us around with a pooper scooper after one of them shat himself through his shorts. I loved him. And playing Inky Stinky Jack, covering one side of a knife with slips of paper, twisting it in the air and making it disappear, learning bridge with the uncle who had bullied my mum throughout her childhood, and watching his beautiful Flake advert of a daughter press her hands together, shuffle the pack through thin air and deal like a card sharp.

I loved going to south Manchester when my parents were away, being treated to gingerbread men by Auntie Renee, playing cowboys and Indians with my sister, collecting September conkers and never knowing how to harden them, sliding down the pole of the climbing frame, waking up to the smell of summer honeysuckle and grass and rushing to the park in pyjamas, eating chocolate crispy cake on Saturdays at Laurence's, watching Noddy Holder's sideboards on *Top of the Pops*, listening to my T-Rex album and jumping off the piano without any clothes on when Metal Guru came on.

I loved the fear of being lost, and exploring empty houses,

Hello Dolly! with Mum's best friend Ruby when Mum and Dad were away another time. I even loved being sick out of the car window after too much Quality Street and steak and chips and mustard. I loved visiting Mum the time she was in hospital having a hysterectomy, then writing her a letter, a progress report, about my thirteen times tables and adverbs and what they meant and how to do them, what a river valley was and how to get there, which of Henry's wives had not had their heads chopped off.

I loved *Budgie* on Friday night and knowing Mum thought it was a bad influence, and Grandma with the blue rinse staring at the telly, legs akimbo, clucking on her Murray mint, pushing it round her mouth louder and louder. Going out with Dad on Sunday morning to Choosacard and clearing the chocolate off the shelves. I loved knowing we had ten packets of chocolate cigarettes and that Dad would light them for me, and that I could squeeze the burnt melted chocolate out through the bottom of the rice paper straight into my mouth.

Knowing friends wanted to come to our house because, hanging up in the wine cupboard that was never a wine cupboard, was more chocolate than they could believe. Running ahead of Mum and Dad, keys in hand, crunching through September leaves on the way back from the synagogue. The late-afternoon extra tuition with the grumbling old headmaster, the stale smell of his books, the aura of a miser.

I loved having baths with my sister in the old days and playing botties to botties and getting excited and wondering why. I loved going into work with Dad and watching the tailor with his needle and thread and fag. Unscrambling his cotton reels and being told that I'd really earned my two bob. I loved the way the crane came the day he moved into the new shop and picked up the gigantic steel safe from the second floor and swept down to the ground. How Grandma re-rinsed her hair especially, and snipped the blue ribbon to open the shop and how I was given a magic card that converted old money into decimals if you held it up at the right angle. I loved the way Dad would drive home and say, you know one day it's going to be you driving me home from work, even though it never was. I loved going to school, coming back from school, going to sleep and waking.

She was right, love did win hands down.

As for hates, there were a few, but if she hadn't asked me to compile the list, probably too few to mention. Having my haircut, the blue zippered cardigan, I hated shitting my pants at Andrew's and his mum asking me, time and again, what the smell was, and wafting air freshener into every hole and corner. I hated the day I started school and John's brother stole my cap, danced around me a few times, and then threw it on to a pole outside my range. But that was a one-off and he only did it to impress my sister who despised him for it. I hated the day I fell off my Chopper after being stung by a wasp, and being taken to hospital and the doctor wrapping up my knee with gauze and Savlon and saying it would be OK. I hated the way my knee went septic, my temperature rose, and eventually my cousin, another doctor, undid the dressing and removed a stone the size of a 10p bit with a pair of tweezers and said, this is why your knee's been hurting so much.

Not many hates for a nine-year-old.

Chapter Three

'Simon, do you think you could just take yourself to the toilet and do a little poo for us?'

No, actually, I don't think I can toddle off to the loo and produce a *poo* in this ice-cream tub to order. No, no, no I bloody well can't. No.

The loos were more patronising than the Sister. You sat there, your bottom hugging the ground, ankles knocking against the last person's misfired piss. Then – now this is the bit I really love, stupid gits – then, you were supposed to push, push, push, wait till your arsehole had begun to open, push push push and then slip the ice-cream tub under your bum just as it was popping out. It took practice, not that you'd want to.

Nurse, sorry nurse, had a bit of an accident, and I've got a squidgy lump of shit stuck to my palm, can you help me?

Sorry nurse, got a spare ice-cream tub, done you a lovely little chocolate whip right to the top, went a bit overboard actually.

Nurse, only chocolate peanuts today, sorry.

Nurse, tried really hard, but I've got a bit of diarrhoea and the tub's leaking, and it's left a little trail from the loo to the ward . . . only joking, Nurse. Well, you gotta have a larf, haven't you, even when you're nine years old, your head's about to explode, you've not seen any friends for a couple of months, you've lost a quarter of your body weight and you want to die. Gotta larf.

Urine tests were a doddle by comparison. At first anyway, till the peeing got difficult. 'Noo, then laddie, can ye just goo and fill this little vase for me,' said the urine monitor, sticking a pint bottle in my hand.

Done the best I can Doc, there's a little dribble, but you can't get a pint out of me.

'Ay, laddie, could ya just go beck and squeeze a little harder. Sometimes it helps if ya pull ye penis first, twang twang back and forth, and then give it a mighty squeeze.'

How d'you explain the implications of not being able to pee to a consultant in a hurry? 'Just a quick urine sample, laddie.' OK Doc, but less of the quick. Can you wait a few hours? You see I'm a little tense because I'm suffering from tension and no matter how hard I try and no matter what I think of and no matter how many people stand outside the toilet crossing their fingers and running the water and reading me *Emile and the Detectives*, and shouting enthusiastically 'Well, Si, is it coming? Any luck, hey Si?' nothing really helps Doc. Could you stick around while I take my dick into the bushes for three or four hours just in case I strike lucky?

I'd been ill a couple of months, in hospital for a ten-day

break. Amazing how quickly you adapt to circumstances. Life was one long shit, piss and blood test. Blood tests I liked. Not the tiny 'just a little prick' in the thumb with a broken razor blade, no they were boring. The one that had me drooling with anticipation was when they came for you with a transparent toilet plunger, bent your arms back and forward a couple of times, dibdibdabbed a bit of sting-as-you-go antiseptic on the spot, and pulled and pulled till your arm was blue and the syringe was full. Two pluses. First, the pain – just enough to momentarily distract me from the drilling in my head. Second, I was convinced that the more blood they removed the more weight I'd lose and soon enough I'd be punctured thin as the boy in the bed next to me.

They took me to a new psychiatrist, my psychiatrist. I may have been half-dead, my eyes screwed shut with the pain, but I could still see she was stark raving bonkers. Fiftysomething, grey bird's-nest hair, eyes straight out of a Hammer horror movie and a silver crucifix that would glow in the dark. I thought she was going to take my hand, lead me to the house of the Lord. Hallelujah! You ain't ill son, you just need a dose of Jung, a tambourine and the good Lord Jesus on your side, Hallelujah!

'Young man, thank you so much for coming.'

If my throat hadn't been mosquito-bite itchy I would have giggled.

'Young man, I'm here to ask you some questions.'

Fire away, I said, looking into the unbuttoned gap in her shirt.

'How do you get on with your mother and father? You have a sister? Goooood. Very goooood. Older or younger? Older, lovely, gooooood. Have you many friends at school? You do, lovely? And, this may sound strange and don't be offended, but do you worry that, excuse me, you are not quite as, well, quite as quick as your peers?'

Ah, that's her game. I knew about this – it was Reg's theory and they had been playing Chinese Whispers.

I told her I was a good runner but I didn't know what peers were. Good, she said, goooood. Gooooooood. Did I find school work difficult? She asked me what I was like at sums and I did burst out giggling. Ouch, my throat. It was about three years since we'd called them sums, and you would hope these people had done a bit of homework, research, I was near enough top of the bleeding year. It seemed so rude of me to laugh straight in her face, so I bit my knuckle and pretended I was crying, so overcome with remembrance of failures past I couldn't speak. I needn't have bothered with an answer though. 'Yes, yes, yes, laddie, don't worry, many children have difficulties with school, work is very hard, very hard, and I don't blame you one bit, not one bit. It's Simon, isn't it?'

Her name was Dr Birtles. She had me down as a thicko, a bonzo, a divvy, a retard.

'It's very difficult to go to school, isn't it, when you're not confident, when you have fears. Do the children pick on you? And, you know, some illnesses, some pains, well you think you feel the pain, but there is no physical reason for that pain. They are called, now don't worry if you can't remember this word, they are called psychosomatic, psycho meaning of the head and somatic meaning . . . well, let's not bother ourselves with what somatic means. But that's the word, anyway, psychosomatic. Now, laddie, if your pains are psychosomatic, can you say that, no I didn't think so, if they are, it doesn't mean that you haven't been poorly or that you need to be ashamed of yourself, or you should feel inadequate. You've not been cheating, it just means that we can start working on the headaches, and if you come to see me a couple of times a week, we can talk together and help them go away. OK? Feeling better now?'

Cousin Steve came to visit. My sister and I were a generation out of time. Dad was virtually fifty when he married, so Steve was fifteen or so years older than me. Gentle, kind, lovely Steve. He would talk to me as if I were his age, he'd even take me to the psychiatrist and while away the time in the waiting room with his bad jokes. 'How d'you turn a duck into a pop star? Put it on the fire till it's Bill Withers.' Liked that one, think he was impressed I got the reference.

He bought me a cassette of 'Don't Shoot Me I'm Only The Piano Player'. I wasn't listening to Elton John though. Nothing personal, it was my head. But I would look at the sleeve for hours, learn the lyrics by heart and, of course, I remembered Daniel from normal life: 'Oh it looks like Daniel, must be the tears in my eyes.'

I was becoming a pop obsessive. Second-hand. The mad thing was that I couldn't actually listen to any of it. I'd stopped watching television and listening to music weeks ago. They just intensified the head nausea. Music echoed and rattled like distortion. At first anyway. Eventually, I think the music and television ban became a dirty protest. So Doctor, you think I'm faking it, well why have I turned myself away from all the things I love? The same with my eating. No one could be healthy and reject food, music and TV.

There were letters and cards and presents from school. Andrew told me how much he missed me, time and time again in different colour pens. It read like a love letter and I wanted to cry. John sent me a little white book on ornithology with lots of pictures and in hardback. Hardback! I must be ill. Laurence sent some chocolate crispy cakes which I couldn't, or wouldn't, eat, but it was a nice thought. It was three months since I'd seen any of them.

I didn't want to see them. I don't know why, just didn't. Maybe I wasn't thin enough yet. Wouldn't it be great if they came one day and didn't recognise me? My sister Sharon visited and bought some grapes for a joke. I didn't eat them and didn't laugh. She asked me what was wrong, said the doctors didn't know, and that Mum had been crying a lot. 'Andrew says they've started algebra and the top group from the third year are all getting special tuition for the eleven plus. You would have been in that group of course,' she said thoughtlessly thoughtful.

Mum bought a massive pad of paper because I told her that I wanted to do a picture. I'd always been useless at art, but now I was desperate to draw. At home, I still had the framed pictures by the bedroom window ledge – T-Rex, Slade and the Sweet. Marc Bolan hadn't had a number one for ages, but he was still the man for me. She bought me *Record Mirror* which enabled me to catch up on all the stuff I couldn't listen to. Slade were getting bigger and bigger – 'Cum On Feel The Noize' straight in at number one. Amazing! Even Bolan hadn't ever come in at number one. And the way they spelled their records was brilliant. In *Record Mirror* it said that Dave Hill had bought himself a car, a Jensen-Interceptor I think, with a number plate Yob 1. Yob 1! Imagine that.

The Sweet were also doing amazingly. I'd liked them ever since 'Little Willy' which sounded so heroically rude. 'But you can't push Willy, no, Willy won't go, try telling everybody but oh no.' Not only rude, but it rhymed brilliantly. Now 'Blockbuster' was five weeks at the top. 'You better beware, you better take care, you better watch out if you've got long black hair.' Long black hair would do me. It was incredibly greasy, weeks since I'd washed it.

Even though Slade and Sweet were having the biggest hits, I was still going to draw pictures of Marc Bolan. Anyway, those gorgeous corkscrew curls were easier than Noddy's and Brian Connolly's. *Disc*, which was like *Record Mirror* but didn't have the BBC charts, said that Marc was five foot nothing. I considered writing a letter to the editor to complain, but my head hurt too much. Everyone knew he was almost five foot six.

After a couple of weeks I'd made about 120 pictures of Marc, and the later ones weren't half-bad. Mum bought me a glitter pen, which helped no end. I tried to do his body once, but that was pretty useless. One of the papers suggested he was getting fat, drinking too much booze and taking cocaine. I asked Mum what cocaine was.

Hospital nights were bloody lonely. All those hours, turning over my stinking, wringing pillows, asking myself whether it could be true about the drugs. As soon as my head felt a bit better I was going to write a long letter to *Disc* telling them they had the wrong man. How dare you say that about Marc, I would start, don't you know he's just bought his mum and dad, Mr and Mrs Feld, a brand-new house with all the money he's earned? That would shut them up.

I'd lost loads of weight. More than two stone. Brilliant. I'd never even thought about weight before, definitely not thought I was fat. But with all this time on my hands I was getting fixations. Two stone! If Andrew came to see me, he'd barely recognise me now. And my face was curry-powder yellow, and my hair almost touched my shoulders just like a pop star. Perhaps I'd get a perm.

They'd started weighing me every day. Out of bed, ice-cream tub and wine bottle to the toilet for tests, and then upstairs, stripped to undies, and balanced on those freezing scales. 'Oh dear me, Simon, under six and a half stone. Really, what's wrong with you, did you drink your banana Complan last night? This won't do, tututut, under six and a half stone.' Yesssssss! one–nil! I thought. Sod you, I thought. Going down, going down, going down!

And then Dave, who would only eat bags of baby peeled prawns, got on the scales. 'Five stone twelve, David, another three pounds lost. I'm not very happy about this,' said the nurse with the face I could have died for if my head had not been on fire. Not very happy? I wasn't very bloody happy about it either.

Dave had become a friend, a rival. He was a couple of years older, the best part of a stone lighter and I felt aggrieved. I suppose there were lots of reasons I stopped eating. No question, I felt sick. Last night when they woke me up at four in the morning to force a mug of Complan down my throat, the nurse with the hairy mole told me it was to make me sleep better.

But there was also the dirty protest, the hunger strike. Perhaps it's inevitable – if enough doctors turn up on your bedside every morning, tell their students they haven't got a clue what's wrong with this chap, if anything at all, says he's got a bad headache, but we all have bad headaches don't we, probably doesn't like school hahahaha! . . . If doctors do this day by day, you've got to try to convince them in other ways.

Then it became even simpler. I was in competition with Dave next door. We were prepared to fight to the death and we had all the time we needed. Dave was lovely, but complacent. He knew he could eat as many bags of prawns as he wanted and still undercut my weight. He underestimated my will power.

I simply refused food. First just dry bread, then nothing. It wasn't difficult. There were other things to think about – nausea and where my body had gone to and why I was seeing the world through the wrong end of a telescope.

After a couple of weeks, I wouldn't even touch chocolate. You would have thought that would have been the first to go, but the boy who used to eat twelve cream eggs a day was ignorant of fatty factors and headache inducers.

I tried to remember what life had been like without a headache, but I couldn't. What it was like not to be aware of carrying your brain, the buzzing at the front, the steel sheet down the centre. I was getting dizzier and dizzier. When I got out of bed for a stool test or weigh-in, I'd have to crawl along the wall. Headache. Pathetic word, it did such an injustice to the pain. The nurse with the soft hands and the lovely baby face and curls under her collar said I could call it migraine, but that didn't feel right either.

I learnt how to vomit at will. Most people know how to do it, but lack the will power. Thumb to the back of the throat when no one's watching, retch retch, retch and the sicky floodgates open. Most of the time nothing came because my stomach was empty. When I refused my four a.m. Complan the staff got nasty. No parents, the other children asleep, it was safe. The night Sister marched over, with her wide hips and sour eyes. She said if I didn't drink it, Mum would be banned from the ward. I drank the banana Complan, all the way down and probably could have been sick even without sticking my thumb down my throat. But I did anyway, just to be sure.

My eyes were playing tricks. It wasn't too bad in bed, but as soon as I got up, chairs and tables doubled up, squiggly lines danced like Pan's People, and I had developed internal disco lights.

'Mummy, my head *hurts*.' She'd become Mummy.

The daily weigh-in, for this relief much thanks. Six weeks in hospital, three months off school, and I was down to six stone. I looked beautiful, absolutely beautiful. Concave chest, rattling tunes on my xylophone ribcage. My nipples were shrinking, my head becoming longer and thinner by the day.

Most of the kids were out of the ward in a matter of days. A quick tonsilectomy, sinus wash-out, appendix job. All anonymous, except for the baby, that poor baby. She was at the far end of the ward, and the nurses were shouting at her parents – it's funny, they'd say, that she seems perfectly fine when she's here by herself. One day she wasn't there and Mum asked why. It turned out that she'd had a brain tumour all the time, and she died, just like that, with the screaming still fresh in her parents' ears. Not even time to say hello, cuddle her in my hollow ribs and ask if she thought I was beautifully thin.

There were three long-termers, chronics, veterans. And what a terrific team we made. Two anorexics and one six-foot-three nine-year-old with gigantism.

Dave, Mark and me. We had a larf. OK, we didn't have much of a laugh, but we were a kind of team, united against the doctors, united in dismay. Occasionally, very occasionally, we'd sit at the tea table in the middle of the ward, play cards, moan about our lot, moan about the tiny kids on the ward. Four-year-olds, five-year-olds, what were they doing there anyway?

Rummy, pontoon, we even tried three-man bridge once,

but none of us knew the rules. Gambling boys, the three of us. We'd play for uneaten chocolates, me desperate not to win. Dave would pour out a bag of peeled prawns, divide them up among the three of us, twist, twist, twist, pontoon. Mark had a lucky hand, always. He'd clear up the prawns and pop them back in Dave's frozen-prawn bag when he wasn't looking.

First time I saw Mark I thought it must be so great. He was posh and confident and he hovered over everybody, doctors, parents, hospital visitors, priests. I presumed he was about sixteen or seventeen and couldn't understand why his voice squeaked like the rest of us. He didn't like talking about his 'condition', although he did say his biggest problem was 'down there' and that he'd need an operation on his brain though the doctors weren't sure if they could do it.

I'd not even considered what lay down there until Dr Barry, the consultant, went on a particularly brutal ward round with his student groupies. There was often laughter, supercilious laughter, nervous laughter, eager-to-impress laughter. Barry strutted along, a self-absorbed dandy, as arrogant as he was incompetent. He always looked as if he'd spent the previous night scrubbing his coat and polishing his stethoscope.

Most of the children weren't worth a stop, but then they got to us. What d'you call two anorexics and a boy with gigantism? Trouble-makers.

'Now this laddie's been with us for weeks. Doesn't like eating, except prawns, that is. We've still got him under observation, but I'll happily offer odds on his condition.

What d'you say, 10 to 1. Pneumonia. Any takers, last offer 10 to 1. Good, no, of course it's not pneumonia, he's not got so much as a snuffle. A wasting disease, anyone? Hello laddie, feeling better today? Still popping the prawns? Not put on any weight I see.

'And then there's mystery boy number two. Seems to be trying to lose weight as quickly as laddie over there. Doesn't even eat prawns this one, mind you he had more weight to spare when he came in. Screams blue bloody murder with headaches, and a sore throat. Here Suzie, have a look down the throat. Not a pretty sight, it's certainly red enough, and you can see where the little mite's been scratching with his tongue? Can't be doing any good. Any offers? Just started complaining about a stiff neck, too. Any thoughts? No, nothing, well it's foxed us too. Morning laddie, what's up? Things can't be that bad. Your face'll stick, harharhar! Feeling better?'

No.

'No, no, where's your spirit, laiddddddddd?' Barry was putting on a show. 'Even if you're not feeling good, just think what it does for Uncle Doctor if you tell him you're feeling a tiny bit better, makes him feel he's doing a decent job. Harharhar!'

Barry marched on with his merry troupe of whitecoats. I wish I'd puked over the girl with the omniscient specs when she poked her finger down my throat. 'Now this one, this one, here's a rare 'un. Morning Big 'Un, how are you today? Now, Suzie, how old would you say this strapping young lad was? Three to two odds-on favourite seventeen, 2 to

1 fifteen? Any advances? Twenty to one, fourteen years old? The book's closed. How old are you, laddie?'

I thought Mark was going to lamp him. 'Come on Mark, get out of bed and put them out of their misery.' Mark jumped up, stood by the side of his bed, and saluted, nine years old, your honour. 'This chap has got what is known in the trade as gigantism. Definitions? Suzie?' Barry continued talking, while he crept round the back of Mark. 'None, just nine years old lad, a fine specimen, aren't you? Now take a gander at this?' Without warning he ripped down Mark's pyjama trousers. The ward was silent, the students were silent, mouths open, one tiny muffled laugh, one sympathetic tut. Mark's dick hung to his knees. He stood straight as you like, stared Barry face on, a tear dribbled down his nose. 'I don't think that was necessary,' he said.

It was difficult to know what to say, so I settled for nothing. Mark didn't say anything either. He went to bed and read comics all day. At five-thirty the tea trolley came round but he said he didn't fancy anything. First words I'd heard from him since the ward round. 'You going to join us, then, on the hunger strike?' I whispered. Had to be a whisper. They would have whipped me back to the psychiatrist in an instant if they'd heard that. He laughed, which was a relief. Dave offered him his bag of prawns.

It was Friday and Sister decided we should be all spruce for the weekend. Not that the weekend was any different for us. 'Bath-time,' she screamed joyously. 'Line up outside your beds.' I got up and fell, dizzy and nauseous. 'See, that's what comes of being in bed too long,' she said offering me a hand.

Maybe the hospital was trying to save on its heating and water bills. Anyway, she decided the operation would be more efficient with two to a bath. Mark and I were selected as team number one, due respect for seniority. The tub was deep and more round than rectangular. I could see him squirm. He couldn't stand his huge legs and arms, but he could live with them. It was his dick, thick as a truncheon and down to his knees, that he hated most. He said the root of the problem was not in his dick but in his brain where he had too many growing seeds. An overactive pituitary gland the doctors called it.

I was embarrassed for his embarrassment and wanted to tell him that I could barely see anyway because of my head.

He turned away to take off his pyjamas, and I slipped into the bath which was far too hot. The pain was nice, a relief. I told Mark it was boiling and he fiddled and time wasted and checked his pyjama trousers for money even though we never had money in hospital. He eventually climbed in and however hard I tried to look at his face, or his chest, or the walls, or the water, I couldn't. I was just staring at his dick, coiled like a Roman candle, round and round, the piss-hole almost as wide as my dick in toto. He had to manoeuvre it into a position of relative comfort, do his curling for himself. 'People always joke about having huge knobs, don't they, lots of lads would like really big ones, wouldn't they, big huge knobs to fuck with, huge fucking knobs that's what the girls want, a huge fucking knob like this inside them,' he said, in a way I'd never heard him speak. Like me, he had no pubic hair, which made it even more obscene. You could have worn his foreskin as a balaclava.

'It's really painful, you know. I can't really explain, but it aches and it sags and it's so bloody heavy. No one would want a knob like mine, not if they knew. No one.' He was looking at my little inoffensive, nothing dick. 'I think they are going to operate on me. But it's difficult, dangerous, and I'm scared. They'll try to make it smaller.' He said he didn't really know what they'd do but someone had told him they had to do something with his balls, split them open and remove some growing seed. If they couldn't stop him growing, he'd had it. His knees stood up like pyramids and clattered together, above my eye level. I asked Mark if everyone was tall in his family, and he said no, but it's a genetic thing, a condition.

It's strange how two separate dirts scum together and separate and create their own borders. We hadn't washed for a couple of weeks – I smelt of sick, he of cheese. I was trapped against Mark, and wanted to open my legs and stretch into the old botties to botties position Sharon and I invented at bath-time. But I couldn't, not with Mark.

'D'you want to spread your legs Mark, you look so uncomfy. Why don't you rest them on my shoulders and the taps, make a bridge.' He smiled and said no thanks. Our scum looked like floaters from the dregs of a coffee cup. I slipped some through my fingers and asked him if he knew who it belonged to. Easy, as with everything, Mark's was bigger, more solid, formica scum.

'When were you first tall?'

'Always. When I was five I was over five foot. At eight I was six foot. It's crazy.'

'How tall d'you think you'll grow to?'

'I don't know. At some point I think you get so tall your head rests in heaven. That's what my Nan says, but I think it may just be a nice way of saying you die.'

'Did you ever like being tall?'

'It was quite funny at first. Other kids were scared of me, and people would want to be my friend because they thought I was tough or old or cool or weird. But then it became so embarrassing. All those people looking up at you, and me always knowing they're just thinking what the bloody hell is wrong with him.'

As Mark relaxed he uncoiled his dick. Just washing it was a lengthy operation. He pulled back the balaclava, cleaning under and over and inside the pockets of flesh, and pulling away his smegma like a decent chunk of cheddar. His veins were exaggerated and the blackheads looked like warts, and his dick was bloated with blood.

Although still massive Mark's arms were proportionately smaller than his legs, and he had trouble reaching his toes. His toes were bigger than my fingers. I put them alongside each other to compare, couldn't resist it. And I smiled and tickled his toes, and Mark smiled too.

I dried myself in silence, wondering what would happen to him if he became so tall that he couldn't walk into rooms.

How did he fit his dick into his trousers? Was the pain, the ache, he had similar to the one in my head. And I wanted to cry for him. And for Dave. And for me.

I used to love watches, had about six, four Timexes, one from Dad and another Japanese Quartz LCD thing. I used to pass the watchmakers on Leicester Road and stare in the window, at the real gold straps and the Rolexes and Omegas and the diving watches with the flashy diver's dials and the automatics that didn't need winding. I thought the uncle that used to bully Mum was so classy the way he wore an identical watch on each wrist – but his military precision was a sham. He had nothing to be precise about in his life. Watches seemed pointless now. I asked Mum to take them home. Who needed reminding of time in here?

Dave started putting on weight. Sharon said he was rather good looking with his face filling out, and how strange it was that now he weighed more his cheekbones were better defined. His hair seemed curlier and blonder and he started smiling, mainly at Sharon. I told him how happy I was for him, which I was. Happy for me, as well, if you must know. His weight was up to six and a half, seven stone, and I was edging towards five. He may have won the battle, but I'd won the war. To say as much would have seemed like rubbing it in. Now that he was stuffing himself with burgers and fish fingers and chips and mash with butter and chocolate milk shakes, I couldn't trust him as before. I kind of loved Dave like I kind of loved Mark, but when he changed, got better, I felt as if I'd won – and I also felt betrayed.

For a week I just lay in bed trying to sleep. I'd taken to wearing shades instead of the patch. Shades and pyjamas. The pain was constant, no better, no worse, a constant drilling of my frontal lobe. Nurses would talk to me. And I'd just hear a buzzing. I wasn't ignoring them, especially not the one with the soft hands and curls under her collar, I simply couldn't hear.

Mark and Dave left. I stopped talking to people, and started to cry a lot. There was a lump in my throat and I could only ease it by crying. I was sucking my thumb more, most of the day. There was a septic scab in the tooth mark. I'd ask Mummy what was wrong with me and tell her it wasn't fair and she'd hold me as tight as she could.

Dr Barry flashed his stethoscope at me and told me I could go home. I asked him why, and he said I was getting better. I knew it was bullshit and said as much. My head was the same, my throat was getting more and more callused, I'd lost two and a half stone and I couldn't walk for dizziness. What's wrong with me? He looked at Reg, old China, Dad's friend, who'd paid a rare visit. Reg looked at me and said you've had a bug, you need a bit of a rest, a good brisk walk and you'll be fine. He renewed his promise to take me down the football to see Franny Lee and said they'll have me back in school in a few weeks. Mum clutched my hands and looked into her skirt. We both knew they were lying.

She bought me a new jumper and platform shoes like I'd never had before. The heels were four inches, the platform three and they were green and brown. My jeans were miles too big for me, so she also bought new cords, brown, with a massive flare and three-button band at the front. I felt so bloody cool that it didn't matter I kept falling over. Not the heels Mummy, I kept saying, it's the dizziness, the heels are nothing. Best of all was the sweater, striped, orange and red and blue and skinny to my chest. Every stripe lined up with a rib. I went to the weighing room, stared in the mirror, so proud of myself. I looked so beautiful. My body made a straight line, I was bottomless, my cheeks concave, huge purple sacks under the eyes, and my skin was translucent yellow. *And* I weighed near enough five stone. If I'd had the strength I would have whooped and cheered and danced all the way down the corridor. As I left hospital, pushed out in a wheelchair, I wanted to shout at everyone, see how beautiful I am, look at me, I'm beautiful.

Chapter Four

They put the punchbag in my bedroom. She said, when you've got the strength, just give it a good wack, and bought me a pair of red boxing gloves to go with it. I'd not asked for a punchbag, but it was a good idea, it made sense. I'd been lying in bed saying I wanted to punch the fuck out of him, beat him to a pulp, beat him to death, and I didn't even have to say who he was. Mum knew. 'I want to hurt his twattish, piggy-pink face so badly, I want to wrap his stethoscope round his neck and pull till the purple veins explode, I want to dye his white coat in his own blood. If he's got any.'

It must have been awful for her. And the angrier I got, the softer she spoke. She must have been playing back the pictures in her head of the little boy who didn't have a bad word for anyone, the little boy who'd deliver her jam and chocolates and hellos on his huge Chopper bike.

Uncle Tom came round to teach me how to box, but I didn't have the strength and I wasn't interested in learning Marquis of whatever rules. I just wanted to hit, and hit below the belt and above the belt and on the head. I wanted to smack that punchbag into submission. Uncle Tom was a doctor, too. A good one at that, but as luck would have it not mine.

Smack, smack, smack, boot, smack, boot. There you go, Barry. Boot, kick, smack, unlucky Reg. Dad walked in and the punchbag was prostrate on the floor and I was on top of it, smack, smack, smack, and I had my platform heels on underneath my pyjama bottoms and I was kicking and kicking and kicking and I couldn't even hear him.

Reg had continued to visit occasionally. His shouting became louder, the veins in his face angrier. He couldn't understand or cope with the idea that he hadn't made me better. He always made the Hattenstones better.

I was becoming weaker, my weight still falling. My brain was watery mash. I couldn't do the most basic multiplications, couldn't follow conversations through, had no interest in anything beyond my bedroom and the pop music that I'd locked out of my life. The letters and cards had slowed down, and I didn't want to see them anyway. Mum said Andrew and John were starting to prepare for their eleven plus and it took me an age to register what the eleven plus was. A few months ago, I'd presumed I would sail through the exam, take my pick of schools. Now I didn't want to know about school. It was an alien world.

I lay there hopelessly persuading myself into my old fantasies. For years I had willed myself into nice thoughts, exciting thoughts, erotic thoughts (even though I didn't know the word) to get to sleep. I'd turn off the lights and dream Mum and Dad had a car crash and I was put in an orphanage and two beautiful, tall, seventeen-year-old Swedish girls came looking for a little boy and picked me. Here in bed, sick, with endless time to visit the impossible, I tried to reinvent the familiar, warm fantasy but it wouldn't come.

Even though I wasn't listening to music I now had this immense, precocious knowledge from scavenging all the papers. At one o'clock every Tuesday Radio 1 ran through the new charts. Mum would listen for me and rush up the stairs with the new top thirty. If there were gaps or mistakes I'd scream, and she wouldn't shout back. 'But is "The Twelfth Of Never" by Donny Osmond or Little Jimmy, of course it's by Donny' or 'Mummy, come back here. "Ghetto Child" is by the Detroit Spinners not the Detroit Emeralds . . . Even I know that and I've not listened to the fucking music for months.' I treated her as a slave, screamed at her for my misery, and she just took it in silence. I don't know where my language had come from. I never used to swear before I was ill, but I took to shitting and fucking like a duck to water. To be honest, it gave me a bit of a thrill and there weren't many thrills to be had.

She must have spoken to her friend Cybil about my language. One day she came round and I was sitting at the top of the stairs and I must have been feeling a bit better because I'd put on my Elton John T-shirt and I was looking through the banisters, saying, 'Mummy, I've got a headache, Mummy, my head hurts. Mummy it's not fair, it's not bloody fair, it's not bloody fucking fair, my head hurts, Mummy.' And Cybil looked up, her face rigid in disapproval and said, 'Little boys that swear get taken to the police station, they do, straight to the police station.' I told her to fuck off out of the house, and Mum apologised as she left.

My record collection was building up nicely. One of the perks of being ill. And every Wednesday and Thursday a pile of papers and comics would arrive to see me through the week. *Sounds*, *Record Mirror*, *NME*, *Disc*, *Melody Maker*, *Beano*, *Dandy*, and Manchester's *The Weekly News*. The articles were reasonably interesting and I learned to read through the language – if a band affected, let me see, 'a profound act of dislocation', it meant they were pretty damn good, I think. My favourite bit was studying comparative charts. Five years ago, ten years ago, fifteen years ago. Even twenty bloody years ago. Twenty years! Twice my life. I didn't know the names of the twenty years agos, nor the fifteen years agos except for Bill Hayley and Elvis. Ten years ago struck a few chords, the Beatles, the Stones, Cliff, a few of them still going. Five years ago was brilliant, all those stars who could have had anything for a year or two and were probably in rehab or cleaning the streets now.

I was reading all about the Beatles. It was two whole years since they split up. Imagine that, more than four times as long as I'd been in bed. They said John Lennon had gone to live in America with his Japanese wife Yoko and that they'd all fallen out with each other over money and managers. Mum told me her cousin used to be their manager. He was from Liverpool and she hadn't known him properly, but his mother and my grandma were sisters. Brian, he was called, and Grandma didn't speak about him. I asked her what had happened to him, and she said he died and it was terribly sad because he was only a young man and he'd done so well for himself. You know, she said, the Beatles were the most famous group in the world. Some people regarded Brian as the black sheep of the family because he had become involved with pop and loved John Lennon and killed himself, but what the fuck did they know?

Auntie Ruby, who wasn't really an auntie, just Mum's best friend and part of the family, had relatives in Hoylake which was almost Liverpool. Ruby came round on Saturday afternoon after she'd been shopping and would tell us the most fantastic, outrageous stories. She even knew the real-life Desmond and Mollie and said it was true, they did have a barrow in the market place. And she was friends with their publicist, a man called Derek who would have been a charmer even without his looks. I asked her what Obladi oblada meant and she said she didn't know but she'd try to find out next time she went to Hoylake. One day I was scanning the *NME* five-years-ago section and felt so proud when I saw Ob-la-di Ob-la-da, and I wanted to tell all my friends, then remembered I didn't have any. 'Mummmy, my head hurts.'

They bought me two new records that had just come out, only they weren't new, rereleases, compilations actually. The 'Beatles 62–66' was their first four years, and the 'Beatles 66–70' was their last four years. The first was red and the second was blue and they had the same pictures on back and front, one from the beginning, one from the end. I could see how they'd grown up. Their minds became more complicated and confused as if they also had steel plates inside their heads. Sharon taught me some of the songs. She went away and listened to them for a couple of evenings and I'd call into her room, what are they like Sharon, what are they like, how does 'The Fool On The Hill' go? And she called back that it was sad and maybe gentle enough for me to listen to, and I said, don't be ridiculous.

Her favourite song was 'Across The Universe' and she taught it to me. 'Words are flowing out like endless rain into a paper cup, they slither while they pass. They slip across the universe . . . jai guru dev a om, nothing's gonna change my world.' And the words were so languid and perfect like endless rain – even though I think I got the words wrong.

I learnt all about the coded messages on 'Sergeant Pepper'. My *History Of Rock* said it was all to do with death, Paul's death I think. And if you looked closely enough you could see all the things that represented death. When I read about how they'd gone to India and found God I felt cheated.

God and I got on just fine when I was young. I went to synagogue once a week, learnt Hebrew, enjoyed the ritual and the kichels and the gefilte fish, drank four glasses of wine on Passover, starved on Yom Kipur, ate fruit at harvest time and threw away my sins once a year. Didn't question the miracles. And then as I began to change so did my relationship with God. Not gradually, a revolution. I decided if God did exist he was a complete bastard.

'Mummy, why has this happened to me? How could a God let it happen? I never did him any harm, never did anything bad, not really bad. So how can He explain it? I hate God, God has fucked up my world and my life and has put me in prison and I hate Him.' I threw out my skullcaps, and mementos from my trip to Israel, ripped up my mini-Sefer Torah, tore up my silver-plated Bible and my Sidur, cut off the tassles from my tallis then ripped it to shreds. I scrawled my hatred on the holy words – God, fuck off.

But even their religious dabblings couldn't turn me off the Beatles, what was left of them. Just before I stopped listening to music I'd heard 'Happy Christmas, War Is Over' and I thought it was the most beautiful, hopeful song ever. Then John went silent. George released 'Living In The Material World', and despite the title and Rolls-Royce and mansion on the cover, it was a spiritual record. 'Give me love, give me love, give me peace on earth, give me light, give me life, keep me free from hurt, give me hope to help me cope with this heavy load.' I may have hated God, but I wanted all this lot; especially to be free from hurt.

I destroyed my framed pictures of T-Rex and Slade and the Sweet. They were still banging them out – 'Skweeze Me Pleeze Me', 'Hell Raiser', 'My Friend Stan' – and I still followed their chart placing, but they belonged to an earlier life. I despised that former life. How could I have wasted so much love and money on gutter glitz?

Yet in spring 1973 I fell in love with Roy Wood and his group Wizzard. *Disc* printed a massive double page spread of him in colour. His hair was raging like a psychedelic furnace

– red, blue, and purple with wild brown roots – and his satanic face paint and brambled beard hid his big Brummy face. He played any number of instruments, produced his own records and had the voice of an angel.

One day when Mum popped out for ten minutes, and I was lying in bed sucking my thumb which was now plastered up and drenched in aversion ointment, I stole out of bed, dizzy as you like, and walked into Sharon's bedroom and took my copy of 'Angel Fingers' which was number one, placed it on the turntable, switched up the volume, and listened. I'd not heard music for months, and I was so scared of what it may do to my head and I was so scared of Mum finding me and thinking I was better that I couldn't really concentrate. But it was just, just, so unbelievably beautiful. I don't know why, but when his voice came in against all those instruments it was like the first footprint in fresh snow. 'Ang-el Fingers, Ang-el Fingers, how I luuurve the things you do-ooo, now it lingers, Angel Fingers, that's why I fell in love with you-ooo.'

For a few weeks I was almost happy. I couldn't remember life pre-illness. I was still puking and sweating and burning, I was still watching life through the wrong end of a telescope, but I had Roy. Roy had just released his first solo album, 'Boulders'. The single 'Dear Elaine' only got to eighteen in the charts, but I wasn't too bothered, although I did write a letter to the British Market Research Bureau politely inquiring whether they'd forgotten to monitor a few shops in the Midlands.

I dedicated my life to Roy. Mum bought me a huge packet

of twenty-four felt tips and every morning after taking that disgusting vitamin chewy and the Haliborange sore-throat sweet and the antibiotics and the Paracetomol, I propped myself up on three pillows, and copied the self-portrait of Roy from the cover of 'Boulders' into a pad. First I'd do the outline, a roundish, plump-but-never-fat face, and the face paint dancing around the eyes and the trickiest bit, the psychedelic hair and beard in Van Gogh colours. After I got the face right, I attempted to draw his hands, their hairiness and the way they grabbed the saxophone like two lovers slow dancing. I couldn't get it.

Wizzard were touring and I was desperate to go to see them. We talked about it every day, but it was a pipedream. She sent off for tickets and said we'll see and I hoped and hoped and almost prayed, but I knew I wouldn't be there. With a week to go, I couldn't think of anything else. I drew more pictures of Roy, and saw myself there in pyjamas, on stage with the lads, playing Bev's drum kit and wo-wo-wo-ing with Roy to 'See My Baby Jive'.

The day came, the Apollo tickets were downstairs and I was puking in the toilet. I was also constipated, hadn't had a crap for four weeks. I pressed in my tummy and felt hard little boulders, an internal tribute to Roy.

Mum and Dad went to the gig. They took a notepad to write down the name of every song and everything Roy said, what he was wearing, the colours that made up his beard. Every time I heard a rumble of car I ran to my window. When Sharon was downstairs watching *Coronation Street* I sneaked into her room and listened to 'Angel Fingers' again, and then I thought I heard her creeping up the stairs and I got so paranoid I scraped the arm back across the record to resting position and ran back to my bedroom with the wrecked single and hid it under my bed.

I was anxious, so bloody anxious. I went into Mum's room to pass some time and took her stool and explored the pill cupboard. My pills, her pills, Dad's pills, family over-the-counter pills. All different colours and shapes, and laid out two of every type in a pair of rows. Eighteen all together. A Noah's Ark of pills. Perhaps they'd make me feel better, or at least drowsy. I emptied the teeth glass and filled it with cold water. I was good at taking pills – practice – and went back to bed wondering whether an ambulance would come with its flashing light. I considered sticking my thumb down my throat and retching the pills up, but I didn't have the energy or interest. I had the best night's sleep in ages, slept through their return.

She woke me up the next day with a big brown envelope. They said it was a wonderful night, that his music was fantastic, and they were almost convincing. I remembered the pills, but I wasn't dead and I wasn't comatose and I wasn't even any iller than I'd been before. Mum and Dad knew nothing about the pills and I couldn't tell them, not after they'd been to see Wizzard for me. They opened up the envelope and poured the goodies on to the table. Unbelievable. They'd been backstage and spoken to Roy and the whole band, and there was the evidence – a yellow badge with a big star and Wizzard in tiny handwriting, a blue and white badge, slightly bigger, with mad Wizzardly writing. And not just autographs on a scrap of paper but a silk multi-coloured autograph book, just for me, signed by the whole band. 'Dear Simon, sorry you're poorly. Love, Bev XXX'. 'Sorry you couldn't come to see our baby jive, love, Nick.' 'Get well soon Simon . . .' 'All the best Simon, . . .' and then at the last, Roy. 'Dear Simon, get well soon or we'll send the boys round. All my love, Roy', and a kiss that looked like a magic Wizzard star. A kiss from Roy Wood, I was woozy and heavy and in heaven.

Chapter Five

It was spring 1973. I asked Mum how long I'd been ill and she said it was almost six months. I wouldn't have known, didn't have a clue what six months even felt like any more. It was both forever and nothing.

One morning Reg came round, sodden with drink and contempt. His breath walked into the room an age before he did, and he was screaming at her while keeping his eyes on the floor.

'You've stopped, haven't you Marjorie, you've taken it upon yourself, without so much as a word with me, to stop giving him the pills . . . Well? Haven't you?' And still his eyes were fixed on the carpet. He'd not looked at me. I don't think he knew or cared I was in the room. Her eyes were red with upset, but she looked strong, and she was staring at him, daring him to look her in the eye.

'Go and get me the pills, go on Marjorie, I want the bleddy proof that he's been taking them. Not that that would be proof. You could have just as easily thrown them into the bin. Nothing would surprise me.'

'Reg, I'm not going to get you the pills, nor have I any intention of lying to you or deceiving you. Can we please discuss this out of the room?' She sounded fantastic, strong as a cowboy, despite her blotchy eyes.

'A few days ago I decided I wouldn't give Simon any of the pills because I knew they wouldn't, they couldn't, do him any good. And strangely enough Reg, that is what I'm interested in – doing him some good, getting him better.' She was making no effort to leave the room – which suited me fine.

'What d'you mean you decided they couldn't do him any good. It's Dr Marjorie bleddy Hattenstone now, is it? So when did you qualify, love? Why not come and be a partner at the surgery . . .' Reg was squealing with anger.

'I know they can't do him any good because I know they're not supposed to do him any good. I'm not stupid, Reg, I can read books and, maybe you'd forgotten, but we've got a couple of doctors on my side of the family. They're placebos. You were giving Simon placebos. And d'you know, could you have any idea, how I felt when I discovered that? My son has been lying in bed in agony, half-dead, and all you want to prove is, he's not ill, he's making it all up. Well, I'm sorry Reg, we're not playing. We won't be able to give you the satisfaction of telling you that your pills have worked a miracle cure and he's perfectly well now, thank you.'

This was terrific entertainment. Now *she* seemed to have forgotten I was there. I didn't have a clue what placebos were, but she obviously didn't rate them.

'Yes, they are placebos. And there's a perfectly good reason for giving him them. After months and months of testing we've found nothing wrong with Simon. Yes, of course, he's had a bug and temperature, but do you realise how many tests we've done, all of them negative. And any self-respecting doctor has to ask himself if there is a reason we've not thought about that would explain his *condition*. And *you* have to ask *yourself* Marjorie why you are so determined to label him as having this or that when to be quite honest there is no evidence that he has anything. Marjorie, I've known Simon all his life, I know that you and Gerry had high hopes for him, and you know sometimes children feel the pressure of their parents' expectations, and they become frightened and miserable and . . .'

'What are you trying to say? Reg, what are you saying? Can you at least look at me while you're talking?'

'Nothing, I'm not trying to say anything . . . it's been a very stressful time, that's all, for everyone but especially you, Marjorie. And perhaps you should, you know, see a doctor, not necessarily me, someone you can talk to, someone who you can tell what a terrible time you've had, someone who can make you feel better in your head . . . a psychiatrist maybe.'

And the room was silent. Reg had run out of advice, Mum didn't know what to say. She opened the door and walked out and Reg followed her and I could hear them walking down the stairs and I could hear their silence, and the front door banged shut.

She was downstairs, ignoring me. Even when I rang the

bell, she didn't answer. I crawled to the top of the banisters and shouted, 'Mummy, I've got a headache, and my throat hurts, Mummy,' and even though it didn't register as a shout she heard and looked up. She said she was sorry, and did I want her to make the bed nice and tidy with clean, warm sheets and blankets and did I want a hot-water bottle and something to eat even though she knew I didn't eat. She was shaky and her words weren't very clear and I wanted to give her a hug but I felt too clammy and I didn't really know how to give hugs any more.

She went back down and the phone rang a few times and she didn't answer. When Dad's car came up the drive, she ran up the stairs into her bedroom.

'Marjorie, are you in, Marjorie?' She didn't answer. Dad walked up to my room, fag in mouth and a bit out of puff. He asked me if I felt any better and if I knew where Mum was. I told him my head hurt and that I thought she was in the bedroom. 'D'you want some chocolate?' he asked, rattling the coins in his pocket and producing a slightly used bar of Turkish Delight. Dad always asked me if I wanted some chocolate.

'Marjorie, are you in there? Is there something wrong with the door, I can't get in? Are you there, Marjorie?' He must have known she was there because even I could hear her snuffling. He came back into my room and asked me if I knew what was wrong and I said no but Reg had been horrid to her earlier, not that there was anything new there. And Dad didn't say anything to me.

He was knocking on the door. 'Let me in, Marjorie, let me at least talk to you, tell me what happened.' He was breathing fast and wheezy and worried.

'D'you know what he said to me? Do you?' Her voice was blunted by distance and tears. 'He said I was the one who needed a doctor, not Simon. And not just a doctor, but a psychiatrist.'

'What d'you mean? What are you saying? Let me in, love.'

'He said I'd been under a lot of stress and they couldn't find anything wrong with Simon and had I ever considered visiting a psychiatrist.'

'He was just being silly. He was joking, love. You know Reg's sense of humour and how his tongue can run ahead of him sometimes.'

'Sometimes? *Sometimes?* You mean when he's knocked back a bottle of Scotch and turns up staggering on the doorstep for a bit of doctoring. When he finally looks at you and draws his stinking whiskery face right up to yours and tells you you're a neurotic whinger who has convinced a perfectly healthy boy he's ill? Is that when? And don't think I don't know about him phoning you in the office for a man-to-man chat about how Si needs a good brisk walk and I need a little bit of *help*. Don't think I can't tell because every time he has spoken to you I can hear it in your voice, the confusion and guilt and suspicion.'

And all I could hear was her snuffling her snotty tears back and him pacing the landing at a loss for words that weren't lies.

'Well doesn't he?'

'Of course he rings me at work. He's my China, my buddy. And he said, mentioned, that you've had a tough time, which of course you have. Let me in Marjorie, let's talk about it.'

'The pills he prescribed for Simon, d'you know they weren't real pills, they were placebos . . . well? Did you know?'

I couldn't hear every word. I was tempted to go and listen at the door but didn't have the energy.

'Does that please you, Gerald? Give you hope that we're going to get Simon better? Do you honestly think that's the right approach?'

I could tell Dad didn't know what to say, but he knew he had to say something. He'd lost confidence in his words. 'No, I didn't know they were placebos, no . . . . All I know is, doctors have reasons and Reg is a very good doctor. And he feels he must try everything and consider every possible option.'

Mum was crying and talking and crying. I suppose Dad could hear her better. It sounded like she was asking him if he thought she was crazy, too, if he thought that she'd made me ill. As she became angrier, her voice recovered its strength.

'Maybe you agree with Reg that I've fabricated the illness, that it's a fiction that starts and ends in my head. Well? Well? I mean, if Reg says it, it has to be true, doesn't it? Reg couldn't be wrong, not only is he the doctor, he's your China, and you could never let down your best friend.'

'Please open the door. We can talk about this sensibly.'

'And the way he goes around telling everyone, especially Barry, that he knew the whole family like no one knows us, that Simon was a second son. And he could see it coming all along. D'you really think Reg knows us, do you? Reg knew *you*, Gerald, but he has never known any of us, not beyond the odd dirty joke and drunken leer at one of your Masonic evenings and a Sunday-morning pat on the head for Simon and how's the football coming on then, young China?

'Did I ever tell you about that day in hospital when he and Barry were hovering over the bed, and Reg was saying to him, in front of both of us, without a second thought, he was saying, "Look at him, you don't need to be a genius to see that he's not grammar school material, and he's got a mother, poor kid, pressuring him all the way to achieve what he's incapable of." And then he'd phone you up at the office and say the same to you. And it didn't matter what he said, it didn't matter how wrong or false or dishonest it was, so long as he wasn't wrong, so long as he'd not failed as a doctor, so long as he'd not failed Barry, so long as he'd not failed you.'

'I don't know what you're saying, Marjorie. I just don't understand what you want.'

'I'm saying that I want Simon to have a new doctor and I never want Reg in this house again. You should be thinking of suing him, not worrying about which Malt to buy him for his birthday.'

It went quiet again and I heard Dad start his car up. He returned a couple of hours later with roast chicken and latkes and blintzers and chopped liver and tongue and hot salt beef and chips – a family-sized take-away for a far larger family than ours. Sharon was at a friend's, Mum's door was still locked, and he walked into my room with his cardboard tray and greased bag after greased bag of stodge. In his hopeless misery he'd forgotten I'd given up on food.

Chapter Six

I'd stopped drawing pictures of Roy Wood, stopped sneaking into Sharon's room for a snatch of Wizzard, stopped reading the music mags. Somehow it all came to an end after Mum and Dad went to the gig and I got all the goodies. My days were empty except for the bloody, fucking bloody pain. Perhaps it was Don Powell's accident, when I thought he was going to die, that triggered it. If the Slade drummer could die, then I could. And for the first time I began to think about death and whether I was simply dying a slow death. Maybe I was already dead and hadn't been told.

I didn't want to see anyone, not even Mum. She came into the room and sat in the corner on a chair and it was pitch black, despite the summer, and she just sat there and we said nothing. And I'd cry and suck my thumb and suck my thumb and cry. And sometimes I could see her crying, even though she'd be asking me how my History of Pop was going or were there any funny cartoons in the *Beezer*. She knew I'd stopped reading.

My immune system was collapsing. Everything going to pot. I was packed off to a new doctor, a neck doctor who told me I had loose ligaments in my neck and that I'd have to start wearing a collar just like my eighty-year-old hypochondriac Auntie Lily. Is that it, then Mummy? Is that what's been wrong with me, that my ligaments are loose? Will I get better once I start wearing the collar? We knew the answer. And I sat in bed with the neck collar on and I could smell Auntie Lily and her stale cakes with the browny-yellow icing. I remembered going to her house, which was all darkness and alleys, and asking her how she was, and she'd say 'dying Simon, dying'. The only time she never complained was when I visited her in hospital and she *was* dying. I asked her how she was, out of habit, and she looked at me and croaked ever so gently, 'I'm fine Simon, just fine.' And here I was inheriting her neck collar.

I had a new doctor, Dick. Dick was my cousin and he came round most mornings. He liked talking to me and I quite liked talking to him, and sometimes – once or twice – he even made me laugh. He told me that once he'd visited the Cavern with schoolfriends and seen the Beatles there before they were famous. And when he said he hadn't even thought they were any good, I was so shocked I raised my head and dragged that disgusting, sopping fringe out of my eyes and asked him if he was joking. Dick was small and fat, a puppy man with eyes full of love and laughter.

The constipation got worse. The stools in my stomach were heavy and constantly achy. Dick brought a packet of suppositories round and asked if I wanted my tummy to get better. I nodded because I wasn't really talking to anyone. 'Can you go to the toilet and stick one of these up your bottom and just sit there for a few minutes?' He handed me a wax rocket and I inserted as requested. I sat and I sat and suddenly there was a ghastly faecal explosion and I thought my bowels would never shut again. The shit exploded round the bowl and off the bowl and up the wall. I was left empty and sore. Mum was waiting outside with a hot-water bottle as I crawled out with shit dribbling down my legs, and she washed them with hot cotton wool and carried me to bed. This became a pattern, a couple of weeks' constipation, boulders in the belly (fuck you Roy Wood), suppositories, then sore and empty.

I couldn't piss any more. Dick said it was stress, he was the one who told me it was called urine retention, and that it was common in poorly people. I could hear voices downstairs and to my side, and they seemed to be in the toilet with me, chanting oh dear what can the matter be, Simon can't even go to the loo and have a pee. I'd go back to bed and return half an hour later and I'd be bursting for a piss. Still, nothing. Eventually I'd force it out, push and push like for a shit and my stomach muscles stretched as far as they'd go and, if I was lucky, a little squirt would burn out. Dad would run water, Mum would make cups of tea, they'd leave the house and wait in the rain because they were distracting me and I'd push and push and burn my bladder. I was going ten or eleven hours without a slash, then a whole day, and I'd go to the toilet and prise open the hole in my helmet with a biro because I thought it would help.

Dick said the only thing was to try a bag, a catheter bag, and they'd just put a little straw in my penis, he always called it penis, and attach the bag like an astronaut and I wouldn't have to think about it again. I cried so long and so bitterly that after a couple of days it was taken away and I was left to my own devices. After a few weeks I discovered that if I went out into the bushes at about eight at night and listened to the owl for a few minutes, and listened to nothing but the owl and thought of nothing but the owl then sometimes it would flood out. And when it finally came you should have seen it; it came, and came and came. And the burn it left was terrible and exquisite.

The constipation and urine retention were accompanied by a three-month bout of hiccups. *Three months.* Whenever I tried to say anything, which wasn't often, I hicked my way through the sentence. And then I got hiccup retention – desperate to come out, but I was too tense. They plied me with books on easy breathing and relaxation techniques but I couldn't read. And where do you find a hiccup specialist? The white dots on my nails had taken over – both fingers and toes were pink-free zones. Oh and my skin was in rebellion – little cuts on my skeletal arms and legs and tummy turned into mangy bedsores.

Infantilism, I think they call it. Like a form of senility for kids. I stopped speaking in sentences and when my thumb got too sore to suck and my other thumb tasted crap I asked for a dummy. I didn't write, read, draw or play – except with soft cuddly toys that I could hug under the sheets.

Mummy I don't feel well.

Mummy my head hurts.

Mummy my head hurts, my head hurts, my head hurts. Mummy I want to go home.

Mummy I'm scared, I'm scared and my head hurts and it feels as if it's going to explode and I'm so dizzy and I can see two of you. Help me, Mummy. Please help me. Why can't you help me? Don't you care, Mummy? Mummy I want to die. Why can't I just die? I don't like it, Mummy, I don't like it. Mummy, I don't like you, Mummy. I want my mummy. Mummy, I hate God, he's a bastard and I hate him. Mummy where's my dummy?

She'd started to feed me, mushed baby food out of a plastic beaker. She'd prop me up, support my head straight as it would go and pray the gunk would slip down. One for Sharon, and one for Mummy and one for Daddy and one for Ruby and one for Dick . . . I can't remember making baby noises, but she insists I did.

[illegible] my head hurts.'

'Mummy, my head hurts, my head hurts, my head hurts. Mummy I want to go home.'

[illegible] [illegible] [illegible] [illegible] Help me, Mummy. [illegible] [illegible] [illegible] Mummy, Mummy [illegible] [illegible] Mummy [illegible] my Mummy.

[illegible] [illegible]

Chapter Seven

The door bell rang and I ran into the bathroom and locked the door. I'd received a parcel from school that day after months of nothing. The messages were sad. Andrew's seemed desperate, almost final – 'I still love you like a brother, Simon, and I always will, and I'll always miss you.' They sent me this massive Airfix Hovercraft, and I didn't have a clue how to do DIY models. I poured all the bits over the bathroom floor with the paints and glues and started randomly sticking them together. Glue, paint, piece, glue, paint, piece. I couldn't even remember what a hovercraft was.

'Simon, Dr Sazenka's here.'

Daddy had told me that an important doctor was coming. He said he was called a neurologist and I thought it was newrologist because he was a new kind of doctor. I could hear him downstairs talking to Mum, asking a lot of strange questions, a bit like a policeman. He seemed more interested in finding things out about her than me. 'Mrs Hattenstone, are you a tidy person? Excessively tidy? No, fine, good.

Would you say you were a worrier, prone to dark thoughts, maybe the kind of person who finds it difficult to get something out of her mind, someone who obsesses? Mrs Hattenstone, would you say you were a protective kind of mother? Before he was ill, did Simon take much time off school?' That was a laugh. Surely, he could see for himself the house was a tip, and as for taking time off school, I was never off school.

By now Dr Sazenka was there waiting in my bedroom, with his bloodhound-in-mourning face and mittel-European gravitas, and I was locked in the bathroom. I began to laugh a hollow disturbed laugh. Mum was urging me to come out and I was so shocked when she began to shout, the desperation and resentment in her voice, that I unbolted the door.

'Do *you* think there's nothing wrong with me, too?' He said nothing, and I was shocked by the seriousness with which he was studying me. 'Well . . .' Still he said nothing. He asked me what the pain was like in my head, was my neck stiff, why didn't I want to eat? And he took notes, and asked whether my neck was sore, and whether the light was painful. '. . . Do *you* think I'm faking it, too?' 'No, I think you are a very sick boy,' he said finally, 'and I want to find out what is making you sick.'

After eight or nine months off school, you start getting letters from the education authority. Bizarre, threatening letters: I don't care if your son is dead or crippled from foot to neck, but he must return to school for the new school year. Of course, I couldn't return to school, but Social Services sent round one of their workers to help me readapt. I would have had trouble keeping up with kindergarten at this point. We met at the hospital. I was crawling and rattling, more snake than human. My hair was way past my shoulders (hurrah!), I was down to four and a half stone (double hurrah!!) and my eyes couldn't focus – a Government heroin warning ahead of my time.

The woman from Social Services took me in her car, which reeked of air freshener, and said I was Simon wasn't I and how pleased she was that she'd heard I was getting better. I would probably have run away from any social worker no matter. She asked me when was the last time I had been shopping and I said a year ago, without releasing my thumb. She asked if I'd always sucked it and didn't Mum and Dad ever take me shopping or for little outings in the afternoon, the Kardomah does lovely coffee and cakes. Mrs Adrian had a theory in keeping with her position – she said people can get very poorly when they are desocialised, and I said de-what and she smiled and apologised. I was so bloody knackered, I couldn't move. It was my first trip not to the hospital since Day Zero and I was slumped against her like a strawless scarecrow.

Let's go for something to eat, she smiled, and I could see the chocolate stains in her upper molars. I looked at her as if she was crazy. 'I know just the place,' she said. 'Chocolate eclairs, donuts, macaroons, you name it, and it's all on Salford Social Services.'

She can't really have been surprised when I ran away, can she? She must have read her notes, my case history. I let go of her hand and ran and ran through the arcade out the other side and I hid and watched and watched and eventually when I couldn't see anyone coming I slipped into the local HMV. I had no money, and even if I had, I doubt whether I would have used it. I just wanted to nick something, to take it off the shelf (they left the cassettes in the tape boxes in those days), eye it up, read the lyrics, once and twice, and flourish it in front of the shop assistant and stuff it down my pants and walk out.

It didn't quite go like that. I was too busy looking over my shoulder for Mrs Adrian. Like most amateur thieves, I was indecisive. Pluck a tape off the shelf, put it in my pocket, take it out, see if anyone was watching, put it back. I wanted the prog rock shelf. Wizzard and pop and singles seemed so trite now. Whereas ELP and Yes and Pink Floyd; even Gong, could tap into the pain of life.

I stuffed an Alvin Stardust tape down my pants and ran off back through the arcade. Breathless, I sat on a bench opposite the eclair and donut cafe. Mrs Adrian ran up, stockings round her ankles, asthmatically wheezing, breathing chocolate fumes. Her glasses were steaming with anxiety. You wouldn't have guessed she was in her early thirties, she looked just as wrecked and wretched as me. I felt sorry for her and even apologised. Yes, apologised.

'Where've you been, I was looking everywhere. Are you OK? You could cost me my job, you know? And I was so worried, and my three-monthly report is due in a couple of weeks. What's that in your hand?' I told her it was a tape by a pop star called Alvin Stardust and said she might remember him from the sixties when he was called Shane Fenton. It's funny, I said, I don't really like Alvin,

I sort of hate him, but I just found myself desperate for this album.

'Where's the HMV bag . . . how did you pay for it?'

'With money, of course. Money I stole from your car, £3.20 to be exact, from the dashboard, two pound notes and loose change . . . only joking.'

They sent me back to the psychiatrist, Dr Birtles, and my cousin Steve came with me again and he asked me if I'd heard 'Goodbye Yellow-Brick Road'. He said it was breaking all kinds of records in the States. 'Did you know "Candle In The Wind" was dedicated to Marilyn Monroe, the girl of my dreams, even though I'm married and she's long dead.' I asked him who Marilyn Monroe was and he laughed. If it had been anyone else I would have slapped him one.

It must have been a shock for Dr Birtles. Six months had passed since she'd seen me, and it wasn't that I looked so much thinner or sicker, although I did, it was that I looked so much younger. She talked to me like a little child and to be honest I didn't even notice till Steve called her a patronising cow. She asked me if I missed my school friends and I said that I couldn't remember their names and I hated school and had always hated school and never ever wanted to go back. She asked me if I thought I'd catch up and I said I didn't care, and that school was for poofs anyway. 'How's Mother? Still . . . troubled?' I didn't know what she was talking about. 'Do you pray, laddie? You know, to God? The good Lord? . . . No, I don't suppose you do. If you offered up a few words to the good Jesus you may start feeling better, you know. No promises, but you may. He's always up there, ready to listen, and He looks after those that look after Him.' Steve told her I was a Jewish atheist.

Dr Birtles was probably in her mid-fifties, her skin unhappy in its bagginess. She talked with certainty, but her eyes were empty and so bloody disappointed with everything. She took out a printed piece of paper from her drawer and said she'd like me to do a little test, an IQ test and I mustn't be worried if I didn't know the answers.

On the way home, Steve told me he'd heard things about her, and I said what, and he said you probably won't believe it. Try me, I said. Every Thursday, he said, she would stay behind in her office and finish off work, work that probably didn't even exist. And at midnight, she'd take off her white coat, and her Jesus-loves-you, tambourine-bashing frock and her yellowed bra containing her sad little pancake titties, and her grey stockings and Jesus-loving smalls, and run into the hospital grounds stark-fanny naked, dancing for Jesus, until security dragged her in. Apparently she would give herself up easily, allow them to take her by her sagging upper arms, walk in head in the air, pop her togs back on and ride home on her Vespa. Every Thursday, and later it wasn't only Steve I heard this story from.

I deliberately sabotaged the IQ test, brilliantly convincing the medical profession that I was a retard. That's my version, anyway. But I don't think it quite worked like that. Yes I was bright enough at school, but it doesn't take long for your brain to turn to mush. Dr Birtles left the room, and I was staring at the questions and they were hard to read because I was seeing double and the lightning was playing up. To be honest, I probably couldn't answer the first few questions, even though they were pretty basic. If a man takes £1 to the shop and spends 75p on toffees, how much will he have left? A hollowed-out circle and the test asked which of three shapes would fit into the space? Three shapes and which shape would fit perfectly into the space? I must have been shocked, I *was* shocked, devastated actually, at what was happening to my brain. And yes, now I remember, I thought I'll rip the test up, just rip the fucker up, and say I'd not even attempted it, because it was so stupid and insulting. Then I changed my mind, I told myself, no, be clever, fail it as badly as you can do, go on, they think you're a retard, so prove them right, just prove them right. I went through question after question looking for the obviously wrong answer, but the scary thing was that sometimes I couldn't even tell which was obviously wrong. After an hour Dr Birtles returned and said, how was it? I looked up and the unbuttoned bit of her shirt, always the same unbuttoned bit, made me feel queasy, and I said to her, I think my head's fallen off, can you see it on the floor anywhere?

Well, said Mum, a few days later, as I was lying in bed, sucking on a dummy because my thumb was too sore. 'Well, you certainly did yourself proud on that one. We've had the results, and they say you've got an IQ of 40, that you're subnormal,' and she burst out laughing. She said she'd listened closely and seriously to everything Dr Birtles had to say and at the end she asked if she should put my school reports in the post.

Maybe, if they think you're subnormal, they'll take you

off the anti-depressants, said Mum. Reg and Barry had put me on the anti-depressants a couple of months back when they couldn't root out a more likely diagnosis. Ten years old and a depressive – some kind of record. 'D'you know what kind of boy, he was?' Mum would say. 'I couldn't think of anyone, not any less likely depressive than Simon.' But they overruled her and said if she wanted her son to get better would she just calm down, please, and take their advice. I was knocking back the Tryptasel three times a day. They never made me feel better, but they did zonk me out, which wasn't necessarily a bad thing. I still had day- and nightmares about Reg hovering over the bed, bawling, 'But there's nothing wrong with you Simon, there's nothing bleddy wrong with you, you're swinging it lad.' Bawling till the red contours in his face were fit to burst.

They did take me off the anti-depressants, reckoned that if I was depressed it may be a symptom of something bigger. I was sent back to the hospital for a lumbar puncture. Just a little prick in the back, said the anaesthetist. Just a little prick in the back, said one of the nurses. But when I saw he was only one of four nurses waiting to hold me down, the steel table and the straps, I knew this would be no little prick. For forty minutes they unsuccessfully tried to bury their fat, obscene syringes in my back. They were slotting a steel girder into my back to match the one in my head. It was just like a recent dream in which I'd died. I'd been stabbed and the blood poured and poured, and dying was just the dribbling away of blood and energy, the residue of an ache.

Chapter Eight

Grandma lived with us for half the year. Half with us, then half with Auntie Jane. Grandpa had been dead four years, his Inky Stinky Jack knife and pooper scooper long tucked away. Grandma had white hair and arthritis, a handsome face hidden under her fierce demeanour. We'd already had one scrap about a month ago. She didn't believe I was ill, I know she didn't, even though she denied it. And I sat in bed and I couldn't get it out of my head that she thinks I'm having them on. So I plotted for revenge. One night I wobbled and weaved into her bedroom when she was asleep, stole her teeth from the glass by the side of her bed, and flushed them down the bog. But they refused to go. I flushed again and again, and still they resurfaced. Eventually I gave up, realising the world was against me and that all my great projects were doomed. When I turned round, red with fury, Mum was standing there in her nightie. She fished the teeth out of the bog, polished them, and put them back in Grandma's glass beside her bed.

But I'd more or less forgotten she was living with

us because she never came into my room and she just sat downstairs in the living room in the equally fierce straight-backed chair with her sticks by her side, knitting for her great nephews. One evening I went downstairs and, from the gap in the door, watched them watching *Nationwide*. Mum asked me to come in, but she knew I never came in.

That night I did. I was feeling peculiar, tense peculiar. I was always more tense when I hadn't cried. I can't remember what she did exactly. Maybe nothing. But I was sitting in her chair and she walked in and Dad said how's about letting Grandma sit there Si, and that was it. 'I never come down here, never, and the one time I do I'm just shoved from chair to fucking chair. I hate you all. And it's my fucking house anyway and what's she doing here, why doesn't she go and live in her own house like she used to. Sitting there, watching us all the time like a fucking hawk, and not saying anything. And just looking at me like I'm the boy with no bastard brain. Go home, you twisted old cow, just fuck off right out of here. And I know it, I know you don't really think there's anything wrong with me, do you? Do you? Do you, heh? Well you can piss right off.'

Mum always said Grandma knew it was the illness talking, my mind playing tricks and she didn't resent it. Anyway, she said, it wasn't that bad what you said – just a mini-strop. She said Grandma loved me. And, you know, I loved her, I loved her, I loved her. And I never told her. And even though she never gave me pocket money or bought me all that chocolate like my other Gran, and even though she always looked so disapproving, I loved her because underneath that terse stiffness she was OK. She cared for us. But it was too late. The next week Grandma moved back to Auntie Jane's and she never came to stay again. Mum said she'd done her six months, it was time to leave. But I didn't believe her.

Mum said Grandma had to go into hospital. It was probably a couple of months later, but it felt like hours. She said it was only for a check-up, and it was, but I knew she'd die and that it was my fault. Every evening when the phone rang I'd hang over the banisters and listen in, and feel such relief (though I knew it was temporary) when Mum said, 'Oh yes Jane, she's fine, just tests,' or 'Sylvia, can I phone you back after *Granada Reports*, Bob Greaves is trying out this amazing electrical car.'

On Friday the phone rang and Mum answered and the room went quiet and I knew what it was. She came up to me and said, Simon, there's some bad news about your Grandma, and she could see I was already crying and so was she. She asked me how I knew. 'Because I killed her, didn't I?' Mum held my hand. 'That's rubbish, where did you get that idea from?' But she knew as well as me.

Me and my cursing. The tongue of death. When it happened the second time I knew it couldn't be a fluke. I became so scared for my powers, my poisoned soul, but I couldn't help myself, I was running over with hate.

Rich boys, hate them, clever boys, hate them, snobs, hate them; doctors, hate them, teachers, hate them, corner-shop owners that sold Complan, hate them, drug manufacturers, hate them; kids in the street having a noisy good time, hate them. Uncles, aunties, old friends, old enemies, strangers, hate the bloody lot of them. Then I turned on butchers. I wasn't even a vegetarian, it's just that I didn't eat meat because I didn't eat anything beside squeezed orange and dessert nougat and mashed banana fed to me in a baby's beaker.

Dad told me he was going to see the butcher about synagogue business. He'd never been religious before. Godliness, well belief anyway, seemed to drain out of me and straight into him. A simple swap. I had never given his friend the butcher a second's thought before.

'How can he? How can he do that? I bet the bastard slits their throats himself and enjoys it and drinks it up from his beaker and dances around a tree naked at midnight. How can you be friends with that bastard, that murderer, that fucking bastard? How would he feel if someone slit his throat? Bastard. I wish someone would. Killer. I hope he dies.'

Dad said what a terrible thing hate was, and he knew it was difficult but couldn't I try to moderate my language. 'If you don't like someone,' he said, 'just say it under your breath, say it in your head, say, sod you, in your head, stick two fingers up at them in your head, but don't let them know, don't give them the pleasure of knowing they've got to you.'

'So you'd say sod you, don't like your attitude, in your head to any old murderer, would you? We're not just talking about Bill Farmer here, we're talking about Hitler. Yes, fucking Hitler. And so long as you know inside your head you've said I don't like you, bastard, that's a good enough reason to keep silent. Well, I hope he fucking dies.'

'Have you ever thought, that being a butcher is a job, and someone has to do it. D'you really think he loves going home smelling of innards and giblets and blood? Bill Farmer happens to be one of the finest, most decent men, I know.'

'Yeh, and he just happens to kill for a living.'

Three weeks later Bill Farmer died. He'd had cancer for two years and kept it to himself. He'd not even told his wife. For two years, he just lived alone with the knowledge of his imminent death. Bill's death terrified me. I went purple when Dad told me. He must have known why, but he never said.

Dad became close friends with Mrs Farmer. She'd come to our house for tea and sympathy and advice on selling the house. Every time she came round I hid in my bedroom. I couldn't speak to her, not after that, couldn't even say sorry, not that she would have known what I was apologising for. I ran away from her and all I wanted to say was, I'm sorry Mrs Farmer, I didn't really mean to kill your husband.

Chapter Nine

Death was everywhere. Except where I wanted it.

I was back in hospital. Ten months on, and the same old routine. Another round of blood tests (the juicy toilet-plunger test) and I was attending the hospital school to catch up on my work. That was a laugh – I didn't even know what work I had to catch up on and couldn't remember what had gone before. In my four weeks, I had a perfect attendance record, read two Paddington books and made twenty-one felt animals. I could no longer multiply or divide, hadn't had an English or history or geography lesson in all this time, but those felt animals really were something and my sewing was coming on a treat. If the hospital had a prize-giving day, no question I would have won the felt-animal prize.

Dad went into hospital, a few miles down the road. For months, he'd been wailing the night away with chronic indigestion and stomach pain, swigging glass after glass of Bisodol. His tummy just went kaput, maybe it was the stress. He needed a double operation for his duodenal ulcer and hiatus hernia. I was given special leave of absence, sick leave, to visit him.

I wanted to buy him a present he'd remember, a real father to son united in sickness number. I didn't have a clue what grown men, anyone for that matter, would most desire beyond two hundred cigarettes. Then I remembered watches. The six cheapo watches at home waiting for me to get better – hidden in Dad's Masonic pinny drawer though I wasn't supposed to know about that. And the watch he treasured, handed down from grandfather to father, and left on his bedside table every night. Well this one could be handed up a generation. Mum took me to Cheetham Hill and we parked right outside Watchman despite the yellow lines.

Watchman's double-breasted window was filled with tickers, from Timex to Rolex. Waterproof, shockproof, automatic, quartz, underwater, diving watches with tortoise shells, he had the lot. Even clocks that woke you up with the radio.

I must have been looking sick, perhaps it was the pyjamas that gave it away. The little Jewish man, around seventy with his trousers pulled high over his swollen scrotum, fetched me a stool and laid out a line of likely watches. When I saw this fabulous gold watch, Timex, £8.50, all my own money, decisive as you like, I said that's it, Mr Watchman, I'll have that one. Is it real gold? He smiled at me, and I thought, cheeky bugger, what are you smiling at me for when I've just paid you £8.50. In cash.

We got to the hospital and Mum fetched a wheelchair,

casual as a shopping trolley. I was wheeled up to Dad in his wheelchair, and it felt like being in bumper cars at the fair. He showed me the scar that sliced through his belly and almost hit his nipples. My Auntie Lena, his sister, with the Elsie Tanner hair and cleavage, took me to one side and said be a good boy and don't do anything to make Daddy feel worse because he's been through a terrible time and did I know how brave he was. The bravest man on earth, she said. I felt queasy, but didn't say a word. Dad reached for a fag and remembered he couldn't smoke, and that he was trying to stop anyway. He was anxious and moody and to be honest he wasn't making that much sense. Auntie Lena went to collect Grandma from the blue-rinse hairdresser and Mum went shopping, and we were sitting there, me in a wheelchair, like Ironside's little nephew, him in his bed.

'It's funny isn't it, Si?' What, I asked? 'It's bleddy funny when you think about it,' and he was laughing and whining like a crazy. 'The two of us a couple of alter cackers.' What's that? 'Old crocks, old cripples. You know,' he said, and he seemed to be looking inside his head rather than at me, 'you know we all need friends don't we, even when we grow up, get older, we still need friends, maybe we need them more than ever. Reg . . . do you remember Reg?' And it was such a crazy question that I felt frightened. He knew, must have known, that every day I thought of Reg and cursed him and smacked him around the punchbag.

'Reg and I were at school together, with his brother, and when I left Heath Street to do the rounds, selling door to door, for Dad, we all stayed best friends. I think we even swore allegiance and cut our thumbs and became, what's it called, blood brothers. And we'd go down the Waterpark, Reg with his university education and me a smart young man with decent clothes and a car, despite leaving school at fourteen, and we'd sit at the bar and knock back the Scotch and talk up our dreams, and the girls would hover by us, and we knew we were a good catch. And Reg used to say, "Go on Gerry, just throw them a glance, that's all they want, just a look," and he used to tease me about what a catch I was and how all the girls liked me, and how Mother thought no one was good enough for me. And he was right, even though I shook my head and denied it. The girls did like me. Even the boys did – but that's another story. And Reg, I suppose he was a shickerer even then, the more he drank, the more sentimental he became. I remember one night we were playing snooker and I wasn't bad in those days, good for a break of twenty or so, and he said, "Gerry, whatever happens we'll always be friends, won't we?" And I suppose I was a bit drunk too, and I looked at him and said of course we will Reg, of course. And he grinned. "Blood brothers, Gerry, blood brothers, we'll never let women come between us, Gerry, will we." And we didn't. There were times when we could have. Funny how things turn out.'

I didn't have a clue what he was talking about and I felt fidgety and trapped in the wheelchair. I could have got out but didn't think of it. And I said, what are you going on about Dad? And I regretted it as soon as it came out because I'd not seen the tears in his eyes. And he was blubbering into his pyjama top and saying, 'I'm sorry Si, I'm sorry.

You know, don't you, I always knew you were poorly. Always. But sometimes things are hard, messy. Loyalties . . . And Reg knew you were ill really. He was just, not exactly out of his depth, he just didn't know what to do for the best. You know kids get better in days or weeks, and he didn't know what to do. But he's not a bad man, not a bad man at all, he's a good man, a good friend.'

And he reached for another fag that wasn't there. A couple of weeks later, when he was back home, and getting better with enviable speed, Mum said to him if he didn't start smoking again she'd leave him. Whenever he visited he showed me the new Timex and told me it kept time even better than his father's Rolex, and I told him it was real gold.

His dad, my grandfather, died before I was born. Dad had lived with his mother and her candy-floss rinse and crazed tidiness, for the best part of half a century, until he got married. The man of the family, the boss. Grandma now lived with Lena, although she had a flat that she never lived in a couple of roads away. She didn't live there because she was worried visitors would turn up and make a mess. It was a showhouse rather than a flat. Once she gave Mum a right bollocking for washing her hands with a clean towel after using the toilet. 'That's what dirty towels are for, Marjorie, and that is *precisely* why I don't live here.' She pronounced Marjorie – Marrdhhhhriee – as if she was flemming up.

Grandma was as generous as she was spoilt. Eighty-one she was when she obediently went into hospital to die. Dad's family didn't do much uncomplainingly, but they died quietly and gratefully. The day before she died I was given more sick leave from the hospital. Grandma wanted to buy me a final present and I went out to choose it.

Even the budgie died. In fact, two budgies died. Joey had shared my bedroom for five years through sickness and health. He was green and blue and had nothing distinctive about him, and never said anything remotely interesting. But we had an understanding. For the past year, Mum had tried her best to keep him alive – changed the sandpaper every day, a new plastic budgie to play with, luxury Trill. But nothing could save him. He died of natural causes, but – I know this sounds big-headed – he missed my laughter and one-to-one attention. I think he died of a broken heart.

Joey was discreetly replaced by Tommy, another green and blue budgie with no distinctive traits. After the tragedy of Joey, Tommy was given all the attention a budgie could crave – one-to-one tutorials, constant company. He flew around the bedroom, perched on my hand and head, I even allowed him to crap on pictures of Roy Wood. The combination fumes of paint and heater finally did for him. Tommy hadn't even made it to his first birthday. We were having the house painted, and I had this crappy old heater in the room because, despite the water bottles and the sweater over my pyjamas, I was always feverishly cold. A year on I still had a medium-grade temperature, which I had written about to Norris McWhirter at Roy Castle's *Recordbreakers* when I was feeling more literary. There was no reply.

The paint fumes were bad news, but the paint fumes mixed with the radiator fumes were fatal. Tommy fell off his perch, had a heart attack. That night I moved into Sharon's room and she moved into mine. And Tommy and I slept next to her non-toxic heater. But I didn't sleep. I spent the night trying to revive him, with love and conversation and mouth to mouth. In the morning Mum told me it was no good, Tommy was dead.

It wasn't surprising that mortality, my own mortality, was playing on my mind. I was visiting one of numerous alleged medical experts, an expert in hiccups I think. I'd never seen Dr Hiccups before and I was mooching in his surgery, and maybe I was being a bit obnoxious, refusing to answer questions beyond the odd monosyllable. Actually, there was a practical reason for the monosyllables. I was incapable of speaking in sentences without the hiccups wrenching apart every word. He asked me to climb on to his sofa, bed-bunk high. The room was dark and leathery as a December afternoon. Dr Hiccups had skin like stone-facing and an aggressive side-parting. He was reading my impressively fat medical folder, firing the occasional question. Perhaps he'd had a bad day, his girlfriend had left him, or he'd accidentally thrown away the hiccups potion he'd been working on for the past decade, I don't know. But he took no winding up at all. He suddenly looked up, intense and angry. He said, all serious and hushed, 'You do want to get better, don't you? If so you have to take advice, you have to want to help yourself if you want the medical profession to help you.' And I suppose I didn't answer because I thought the question was so bloody stupid, or I may have made a wanker's circle with my thumb and index finger. But he had a momentary lapse, he couldn't help himself, and it was out, just like that, and he couldn't take it back.

'D'you want to die, Simon, d'you actually want to die?' And I couldn't believe it, I couldn't believe a grown-up, a doctor, had mentioned that taboo word, the one that was banned from my presence. I wanted to hit him and hug him.

'Do you want to die?' I couldn't say anything. I had a basketball in my gullet. Do you want to die? So it has come to that? Those are the stakes. That's what we're playing for. I returned to my ward bed and turned towards the wall. I shut my eyes and thought about it, Do I want to die?

I'd said the word often enough. But it was just a word, not, you know, death, blankness, absence, the end. A death sentence. Why had it taken so long to work out? After all, I'd never imagined myself getting better, that seemed beyond question. And I knew I couldn't remain sick, sick, sick all my life, with no movement either way. And if the movement wasn't upwards, it had to be downwards. And if it was downwards, how much lower could it get than now?

No, I didn't want to die. I had hope. I can't explain what the hope was, it wasn't specific, but I knew life didn't have to be so bad. I didn't want to die. But I couldn't stop thinking, is this it then, when Mummy and Daddy and Sharon kiss me good night, is this it then? The last good night. The last kiss. From then on whenever I woke up, often in the middle of the night, I'd pinch my arms and legs, I'd pull my fingers back till they hurt and put my hand in my pyjama trousers and feel around for sweat, I'd speak to see if I could hear myself. When I tested positive I knew I was alive. Then it struck me that maybe in death you can still feel and talk and hurt, and maybe it's just other people that cannot hear you or feel your pain. And maybe I was dead already, but there was no one here to tell me. Maybe part of death, the cruellest bit, was working out that you *were* dead.

I began to pray, even though I had no intention of renewing my belief in God. The coward's way, backing both ways. I prayed every night in my head, through the lightning and drilling. 'God, I don't know if you exist and really I hope that you don't, and if you do I think you're an absolute bastard for putting me through this, and if you're supposed to be a God of love as people say, how can you do this to me, and Bill Farmer, and Joey and Tommy and my two grandmas and Brian Epstein and Mick Jones and Jimi Hendrix and most of all me, you bastard. But if you do exist, please please let me live, don't kill me, God because I want to live and be happy and better, you vicious twat. Amen.'

Chapter Ten

Mickey came out of the blue. He wasn't called Mickey when they brought him home, but it was inevitable. The only dog I'd known was a Mickey. He belonged to Auntie Renee, a West Highland terrier who spent his life on his hind legs performing for chocolate buttons. Our Mickey wasn't much of an entertainer, not like that anyway.

Dad and Sharon went down to the kennels. They were even more ignorant of dogs than me and Mum. We had a tiny hardback guide to pedigrees at home which I kept by my bed, and even though I knew nothing about real dogs, I could name the different types like cars or pop bands.

Mickey was liver and white, loopy and so tiny he couldn't climb the first stair. Every time he fell back and rolled over and tried again. He was only six weeks but already had a growl. He growled with pleasure when tickled behind his ears, with anger when he couldn't make the stair, with self-pity when he shat out his worms like a king-prawn bhuna.

They said he was for me, my very own dog, a present,

and he'd help me get better. I don't think Mickey had been told though. The people at the kennels said Springer Spaniels would be perfect because they were steadfast gun dogs and intelligent. They didn't bother mentioning that they are also anarchists. Mickey decided all food was for stealing (that didn't bother me), posh sofas were for peeing on, carpets were for shredding and I was for mauling.

Years later he became a local celebrity, Mad Mick, banned from the park for catching ducks. But there was always integrity to his madness. And anyway the ban was pointless because Mickey couldn't read the sign on the gate. He was stocky with elastic muscles and a great sense of injustice. For years he was taunted by a psychotic boxer and his demented owner – they stood on the road outside our house, Sam saying come on Mickey, come on, come and have a go if you think you're hard enough. And Mickey's tail would stick in the air like a bog brush, and he'd yelp his uncertainty. Eventually, he did have a go and he beat Brut senseless. The same with another big dog, Chad, who belonged to the nunnery and wandered free, raping and bruising his way round the park.

Me and Mickey, two crazy, angry boys fighting over the same territory.

We quickly grew to resent each other. Mum said he could feel that I was different, that he wanted my love and time and knew I wasn't prepared or couldn't give it to him. So I made an effort. I couldn't take him for walks or run after him in the park or play football with him, but I could give him his Chum and brush his coat clean of fleas. Auntie Renee taught me special ways to tickle dogs into submission – under the ears, and his head would waver and his eyes would roll ecstatically, or under his hind legs and he'd roll on his back, legs vibrating, like a dying wasp. Quality time, that's what he needed. What we both needed.

So I came down and sat on the big square fourth stair and I'd say, come on Mickey, come on boy, come on my dog, my love. With his black floppy ears he looked like the French footballer Pierre Rocheteau. He ran up and I cuddled him and we rolled over and I thought we were playing, but he was biting and his paw nails were extended in a threat. He clawed through my pyjamas, ripped them to shreds like he'd ripped the carpet, like he ripped into Chad and Brut. My legs were raw, pyjamas hanging off my legs and arms and I was rolled into a weeping foetus. He stopped. And he licked me, and Mum said she thought he was trying to say sorry. Dick gave me a tetanus jab in the bottom which was heavy but painless, and I returned to bed. Dad suggested we could give the dog away if he was upsetting me, and I said no because he was mine and he loved me and was just having fun, although I knew there was more to it than that and that I was just going to keep myself to myself from now.

I'd gone full circle, almost a year had passed. It was October 1973 and the afternoon autumn light was playing painful patterns in my head. The woodpecker curtains gave me nightmares and I wanted Mum to get rid of them, but never got round to asking her. Time had become such a mystery. I never understood what I did with the days, how I made them pass, how I occupied my mind for the eighteen or so hours I was awake. Hours, minutes, seconds, so tedious, repetitive. I needed a subdivision of seconds. Yet a year had gone just like that. I suppose my mind didn't need occupying. It was already occupied. There were days when I just stared at the woodpecker curtains, watching the light shade brighter and darker as time moved on and away. All things must pass, but this didn't, it was a lie or a daft hope, propaganda, the talk of priests and rabbis. So I decided to destroy the George Harrison record, 'All Things Must Pass'. It wasn't easy because of the boxed set, but I managed, turning the corners of the box-cover up, loosening the angles and then slashing away with scissors. I bent all three records till they snapped.

Auntie Renee bought me a little plastic dog, a Dalmatian attached to a rubber pipe and an air pump. Every time I pumped, the dog jumped. The dog sat on my bedside table and the tube just about stretched to my bed, and for days the dog would jump into bed and off the bed. Sharon bought me some jumping beans in a transparent tube, but they didn't work on the soft surface. Renee also bought me a glass bird whose head nodded back and forth and back and forth into a beaker of water. Eight hundred nods represented an hour. I worked that out. And one day I told the time from seven in the morning till *Coronation Street* by nods, and shouted down at seven-thirty p.m., Mum is *Coronation Street* starting? And she rushed up and said, yes, how did I know?

Her skin was flaking and there were red dotted circles round her neck like tiny knife imprints. She took out her book of photographs from the early fifties when she was in her twenties, single and brave. Teaching in Scotland and kibbutzing in the new state of Israel. Pictures of her, arms round her feisty idealist friends, pictures of her and the Morris Minor and five disabled children and a couple of folded wheelchairs, pictures of her with shades on, her legs looking surprisingly long, and her beautiful, imperfect face laughing into the camera. She told me how she'd stopped working when she got married and how she was quite old to be a new mother, even though she was only in her early thirties which is nothing now. 'Before I knew it, Sharon was born and you were born, and both of you were at school, then you were ill, and I'd not even had time to think how much I missed those little kids with their wheelchairs and dribbles and dependent love. When I was in bed after the hysterectomy I thought of those weekend trips to Ma's house when one of the kids would invariably swallow the dregs from a bottle of Dettol or Vim and we'd pile the folded wheelchairs into the car and head off to the nearest casualty.' And Mum was smiling through her memories.

We looked at pictures of her wedding, and the white dress and the non-existent bust. She said how strange it was when it came with pregnancy, and she'd not even had to wear a bra all those years ago, and now here she was a 38C worried about menopausal sag. Pictures of her and Dad, still bald but thin and svelte. You could see why they said he had a good eye for clothes; and on holiday, surrounded by a satellite of friends, and the other women looked so complacent and dead-eyed. And still she stared defiantly into the camera with her big brave beautiful face, delivering a silent monologue, 'What am I doing here when I could be making myself useful?' Reg and Beth and Eve and Sam, Mum and Dad, and Reg's brother chewing on a boastful cigar at a function, probably Masonic. They'd all obviously had a bit to drink, especially Reg, whose arms looked as if they were about to slip off the table. He was smiling deep into Mum's cleavage and Dad was toasting the future.

She showed me the St Christopher a friend, also a teacher, had given her years ago, before she met Dad, and she told me that she thought he loved her and in a way she loved him, but there was never any question of that kind of love, and everyone was surprised he lived into his thirties. He wrote her love poems. There was a photo of Mum and a tall, wiry man with round National Health specs. She was looking at him, her arm brushing his, his kind, unhappy face shied away from the camera. I asked who he was, and Mum said, oh just a man I used to know in the old days, we were close friends a long time ago. He was such a clever man, but his cleverness never made him happy.

Mum was in her mid-forties, and allowing the colour to run out of her hair. 'My hair was jet black,' she said, 'jet black, just look, but it started to grey in my mid-twenties and that was devastating, so I dyed and dyed.' And now the white-metal roots bullied their way past the black dye and she didn't care. Like she no longer cared that her clothes were old and aged her. So what if they said at Dad's shop, 'Isn't it funny that Mrs Gerald has got free rein, she could have anything she wants from the Women's, any frock, any suit, and she just slumps around the house in those nylon trousers with the elasticated waist and a British Homestores sweater.' So what? Mum didn't care and she knew they weren't bad people, and they'd say it quietly and briefly, and probably scold themselves afterwards for their insensitivity.

One day when Mum had gone shopping in Cheetham Hill I went over to her dressing mirror drawers and pulled the St Christopher out of the envelope. There was a photograph in the envelope, sepia and frayed, of a man with his hand round Mum's waist. He was tiny, almost a dwarf, and his back was bent like a half-moon.

I looked in the mirror and my face had changed. The expression was blank as a baby. There was hair growing between my eyebrows, on the bridge of my nose. New hair, like the stuff I was getting around my dick. And two symmetrical moles on my chin, with a couple of wild hairs sprouting from each. I took her tweezers and plucked the hair from the bridge of my nose. I was prepared for the hurt, but it felt nice and left a pinprick and red marker. I plucked the hair from my moles, and that hurt. It came away slowly, the whisker leaving a white fleshy residue clinging to the root. I was so preoccupied I didn't hear Mum return. She walked in and asked what exactly I was doing. She said it was a woman's prerogative to pluck facial hair, men didn't do it, let alone boys.

I asked her if we had any of our old toys in the living-room cupboard.

'You mean, the toys you played with when you were

babies?' She brought me a couple of dinky cars I'd not seen since I was five – a Hillman Imp and, much more exciting, a Batmobile, squeeze the boot and it motors off by itself. I buried my head under the sheets with it. The cupboard was crammed with distant memories. Rubbery snakes, the doll that spoke when you pulled a string, a furry frog with pop-out eyes, colouring in by numbers book, Paddington Bear with a marmalade sandwich under his red hat. All joined me under the sheets.

Occasionally I thought of people I'd not seen for a long time – apparently Andrew had given a talk about me at school, and he said I was so poorly that no one, not even him, could see me. He asked everyone to pray. *Pray for me!* Silly fucker. The piano in my bedroom had been sold, not for much. I was tempted to ring Laurence up, after all this time, and ask if he'd found anyone else's piano to jump off naked to the sound of Metal-Guru. The look on his brother's face the day he walked in and we were there, both of us, stark-bollock naked, mid-air diving on to the bed. Dave and Mark, my hospital team-mates from the early days, had become part of the collective past, so I saw them alongside Andrew and Laurence and John, even though they belonged to different worlds. I bet Dave had put the pounds back on. Had Mark had his operation?

Andrew, Laurence, John, Mark and Dave . . . I'd shut my eyes and they almost turned into social occasions, visits. I saved them for the night when I couldn't be disturbed. I was convinced people could read my thoughts and fantasies, and I'd be exposed for 'receiving' visitors.

I also did my reading through the night. The light was easier, softer, a penumbra. I didn't want to go to sleep. If you don't go to sleep, you can't die.

It must have been about two in the morning and although I wasn't reading the music mags like I had been, I'd started on the *Beano* and *Dandy* again. I was also reading a comic Sharon used to get years ago called *Twinkle*, which often had little presents on the front – bangles or rings. I was developing a taste for jewellery, costume jewellery.

I was reading 'Dennis the Menace' on the loo and trying to have a wee. Pushing and pushing and nothing was coming, so I gave up for a bit and concentrated on the comic. Everything had turned out much better than expected and for once Dennis's dad was chuffed with him. Dennis said to him, 'See Dad, I'm not just an ugly face.' *I'm not just an ugly face! I'M NOT JUST AN UGLY FACE!!* I couldn't believe anything could ever be so funny. A chuckle became a laugh, a laugh became laughter, laughter became hysteria. I was stamping my feet with joy. I turned on the landing light hoping it would wake Mum or Dad up, but it didn't. So I ran into their room and I couldn't control myself. 'Mummy, Daddy, Mum, Dad.' She asked what it was, was I upset and did I want to come into bed for a bit?

No, I said, no, I'm laughing. Look at this, it's unbelievable, it's just such a brilliant joke, and I tried to tell her but I couldn't because of the hysteria. I tried again and creased up again. And I felt that burning sensation in my dick and thought my pee was going to come, but it didn't matter really because this was just so bloody funny. Dad asked if it could wait till tomorrow and I said no, it bloody well can't. She turned on the light and took the comic and I showed her the bit. She was still half-asleep, and she read it and looked at me, and I was still creased up and she laughed as long and loud as me.

My mouth was almost as painful as my head. I'd given up on the Haliborange and the million and one assorted pastilles ages ago. Temporary relief came from scratching my throat with my tongue. But the more I scratched the worse it became. I rolled my tongue back and felt the hole in the top of my mouth, and I could fill the hole with the tip of my tongue and scratch. My mouth was septic, tender as pastry.

Once every couple of weeks Steve came round to take me to the psychiatrist's, still batty as hell, the Jesus tambourines and the open-button gateway to her titties. The visits had become routine – she asked me if I'd always been so close to Mum, what was my favourite food, why did I keep running away from the social worker in Salford Precinct (it had become a habit, a thrill), did I ever think of school, and was I sure Mum didn't want to come and see her by herself? At the end of every hour, she'd hitch her glasses on to her forehead, tap the desk, and say, Well we're not there yet, but I think we're making progress. She only once mentioned the IQ test. 'You *were* trying, laddie, weren't you, trying your very best, weren't you?'

The first few visits after Steve told me about her running routine were almost fun. She would talk and I would turn off, watching pictures in my head of her running around the yard, flop, pant, flop, flop, pant. But it lost its appeal, my imagination was a pot of mushy peas. I just wanted to lie down and cuddle something soft and non-human.

We normally sat and waited in the psychiatric department and Steve cracked bad jokes and winked at me about her streaking. But this time she was waiting for us at the entrance, hands spread across the doors in an exaggerated gesture. Back off, she seemed to be saying, back off. I thought she'd had one of her turns and was waiting for the ritual strip. The shrill wind was rushing through her unbuttoned shirt, leaving her more exposed than normal. She looked clammy and flustered.

'Mr Hattenstone,' she said in a frenzy, 'Mr Hattenstone . . .' Steve told her he wasn't Mr Hattenstone, not my dad, never had been, and wasn't it pretty bleeding obvious?

'Mr Hattenstone, outpatients have sent me test results. They show Simon has a virulent, more virulent than we've seen in a long time, a virulent streptococcal infection. It's terribly infectious, terribly. We don't want to see him here again, ever. Not in psychiatry. It seems apparent that his problem is physical rather than mental. And if you could please drive him home and inform your consultant about the next step because Mr Hattenstone, I'm afraid the lad is simply too infectious to have on the premises.'

Chapter Eleven

Oh yes, oh yes, oh yes, oh yes, oh yes, oh yes, oh yes. Revenge is mine, one–nil, we beat the bastards one–nil, we beat the bastards one–nil, we beat the bastards one–nil. I am poorly, I am poorly, I'm so poorly, yes I am, I am poorly oh so poorly, I am poorly, yes I am. He is poorly, he is poorly, oh so poorly, yes he is, he is poorly, incredibly poorly, he is poorly, yes he is.

Ecstasy is a streptococcal infection, not just any old streptococcal infection, but a malignant, nastier-than-thou infection, a killer infection, an infection to die for. I couldn't believe my luck, I was in seventh and eighth and ninth heaven, really truly madly fucking ill, and no Barry, and no Reg and no mealy-mouthed bastard relative could deny it.

We were driving home in Steve's Hillman Imp and I was drumming on the sideboards and grinning like an idiot. So I felt crap and my head was pounding with lead hailstone, but it didn't matter. We could hire a full-scale choir and I could conduct a gala evening of songs rewritten in celebration of my condition.

'I am poorly, I am poorly, I'm so poorly, yes I am, I am poorly oh so poorly, I am poorly, yes I am. He is poorly, he is poorly, oh so poorly, yes he is, he is poorly, bleedin' poorly, he is poorly, yes he is.'

I yelped and jumped into Mum's arms and screamed and jumped out of her arms and ran down the street. 'He's so sick it's unbelievable, he's so sick it's unbelievable. So Mama, weer all crazy now, oh yeah, I said Mama, weer all crazy now. OK, out you come, anyone who thinks I'm not really ill, come on, Mrs Leotard I know you're there. Don't be shy. Come on Barry you bastard, what have you got to say now, come on fucking Barry, come and see me now, you bastard. And you Reg, let's be having you, bastard.'

A couple of neighbours came out to watch for confirmation that I'd flipped, but most of them scraped back the curtains and enjoyed the performance in the privacy of their own home. And I didn't give a merry shag. And you know what, I don't think Mum did. And you know what's more, I don't think Dad did that much.

Fuck you, I'm ill. Here's the certificate. Woooooooooo-ooooooooooooooooooooo!

Yeeeeeeeeeeeeeeeeeeeesssssss! I'm ill. So fuck off with your mad psychiatrist and your education officers and your Freud and your Jung and your fucking fuck.

Then came the triumph of triumphs, double top, double bogey, double diamond. Dr Sazenka rang up and said the indications were that I had viral encephalitis. Different tests, different results. All passed with flying colours. The brain scan and encephalogram seemed to have done the trick. I had thought it was pure spite when they made me drink pint after pint of water and then sweat and burn the piss out, but now it seemed a tiny sacrifice.

He wanted to refer me to a new paediatrician, Dr Connolly, and asked, would I go into hospital for a brain biopsy? Viral encephalitis. I didn't have a clue what that was, but I was ecstatic, it sounded wonderful. Would I mind having my head split open and examined? Course I wouldn't mind. It was the least I could do for them. I asked Mum what viral encephalitis was and she said it was inflammation of the brain. 'Does that mean I'm completely fucking doolally?' I asked victoriously.

bed thought it was pretty sporty, when they moved on the [illegible] [illegible] pint of water and then [illegible] and [illegible] the [illegible] [illegible] [illegible] [illegible]

[illegible] [illegible] to [illegible] [illegible] [illegible] [illegible] [illegible] [illegible] [illegible] [illegible] [illegible] [illegible] [illegible] [illegible]

Chapter Twelve

I was Prince Charles and the Queen Mum rolled into one. In a new hospital, propped up with fresh pillows, brand-new collar, new throat swabs, new syringes, new Complan, new CAT scans, new suppositories, new doctors, new nurses, new positive reinforcement techniques, new throat lozenges, new anti-inflammatories, new lumbar punctures (just a couple more, and nowhere near as painful), new faecal tubs, new urine samples, new headache pills, new hope. And an operation. An op! Oh, the glamour of it all. I lay snug in my new-found glory, flashing my passport to credibility. And what is wrong with you, young man? Well, actually, I have a virulent streptococcal infection, so virulent they banned me from the last hospital, and my personal neurologist has good reason to believe I may be suffering from viral encephalitis, a very rare condition indeed. So rare in fact that most people have not heard of it, including it would seem most members of your honourable profession.

The op was on a Tuesday, the day the new pop charts

came out. I celebrated the streptococcal discovery with a first open listen to music in fourteen months. A glorious day. It wasn't as if anything had changed internally – my head was still crumbling like one of those documentaries they show of a high-rise block being blown up. The road workers were drilling away, the lightning was blasting its way along the meningal heath. But my conviction overwhelmed everything else.

I asked Mum to bring a radio into the hospital. There was no fanfare, no dramatic drum roll, because no one knew history was being made when I turned the tranny on and heard, for the first time in more than a year, Tony Blackburn and his terrible jokes. Nothing had changed since I left the world – the hairy cornflake DLT was still there, as was Johnny Walker and Diddy David Hamilton and Annie Nightingale and music-loving Johnny Plee. And I was disoriented by the sameness. I'd presumed the revolution wasn't simply in my head, that I'd come out to an equally unrecognisable world.

Operation Brain Day began like any other morning. I woke at six and I pinched my arms and legs, pulled the new hairs on my legs, and I tried to talk, and gently bit into my palm. I decided I was probably alive although I knew I could never prove it. Then on to the internal philosophy class. Was this really happening to me? Not the op, but the past fourteen months. I closed my eyes, opened them again, closed and opened and accepted the starched hospital walls as reality. A perfectly normal day in the life and living death of Simon Hattenstone. Except for the giddiness of hope.

Dr Connolly, the paediatrician, was speaking to me. His words massaged me. I was baffled and couldn't work out why it felt so alien. He told me that Dr Sazenka would operate on me and exactly what would happen in the theatre. First, they would put me to sleep with gas and then when they were sure I had nodded off, they would drill a hole in my head and have a good nosy. They'd stitch me up, ten stitches should do it, he said, and you won't believe the smell when they take them out. 'I thought I better warn you about that but that won't be for days yet. So they'll stitch you up and push you back to the ward and a couple of hours later you'll come round. You will probably feel dizzy and lost and maybe nauseous. But don't worry, this is perfectly normal. And you probably won't want to eat. For a few days the nurses will leave a bedpan beneath your bed and whenever you need the toilet you call them for help. You do it in bed because you won't have the strength to go to the toilet. Now good luck and be brave and make sure you don't eat anything for six hours before the operation.' He spoke with those lovely watery eyes, looked straight at me, and I knew that for some reason he did care.

This was heaven. Not only an op and a consultant who treated me like a human, but I didn't even have to eat or drink. I may be back down below five stone after this lot, I thought, and what then? What will be the outcome? It's an operation, so I will be better, yes? But I didn't want to ask Dr Connolly such an ignorant question when he was treating me like a friend.

A show-off porter boy raced the wheelchair down to

the theatre. That was a fun start to my big day out. The surgery walls were snot green, and lit up by transfers of Mickey and Minnie Mouse. Alongside the cartoon characters hung electric drills, bigger, more ominous than anything you'd find at the dentist. Hanging on one of the drills was a lime-green mask, the gas mask.

The anaesthetist strolled over, right leg forward, flick, left foot forward flick, head jutting back and forward like a chicken. He chewed his gum vigorously and contemplated a bubble till he remembered he was in theatre.

'Have you ever had an operation before?'

'No sir,' I answered apologetically. I don't know why I was in awe of him. 'We'll slap this over your face and before you know it you'll be asleep and the operation will have started. We'll drill a little hole in your head and have a good look inside your head. Don't worry, I can see you're a bit peekish, you won't feel a thing because you'll be asleep – we hope! No, that's just my little joke. I bet you won't even remember that you've been away, and you know what the best thing is, the best thing is you'll have this cracking scar like an anchovy to show your friends.' Friends! As if!

I was left alone in the theatre for a couple of minutes, staring at Mickey and Minnie, who were pulling faces at me.

The gas didn't work. Not at first anyway. They told me it would take a few seconds, and I was kicking and cursing and telling them I wasn't going to sleep. It was only when they strapped my head into the mask that I became frightened. I shouted for Mummy and kicked some more and a couple of nurses held me down by my legs, and

Mickey and Minnie were wagging their fingers at me and pulling their exaggerated ears, taunting me. What will they find? Will they take out pieces of brain and wrap them in popping paper?

'I want my Mummy. Mickey. I hate you Minnie, Mummy, help me. Fuck you, God.' And in my delirium I was bound for purgatory, the price of my cursing, the small-minded bastard God.

They admitted it, told Mum they'd not anticipated how much gas I would need and she just said my resistance to everything had built up, even gas. Dr Connolly told her the operation had been a success and, sure enough, they had found little antibodies splattered on my brain like cotton tadpoles. He couldn't see the infection, he said, but if there were antibodies there had to be an infection.

When she told me I was glad, but too sick to be ecstatic. I don't actually remember coming round, but I do remember a nurse – cuddly and soft and pink and Irish pretty – looking into my face. My vision was distorted, even more than normal, so I could just see a long skinny, bony face, bulbous eyes, and it reminded me of pictures Mum had shown me painted by a German man who thought everyone grotesque and deformed. 'You've had an operation,' she said.

'Where's my radio?'

'You don't want a radio now, love, you need rest. Everyone needs rest after an operation. Especially a big one like you've had. D'you know they put ten stitches in your head? *Ten* stitches.'

'But what time is it? It's one o'clock, isn't it? One

o'fucking clock and it's time for the charts and I bet because of you I've missed them, and I've waited all bloody week for them.'

I wasn't fit for such an energetic tantrum, the sweat on my belly and bollocks was rising and the groadies in my throat revving up. She was kneeling over, placating me, and I did try to hold on and call for a bucket. But it was too late, and a parabola of watery vomit shot out of my mouth, on to her hair and down her glasses. I couldn't help it, honest, I didn't even know it was happening. The nurse whimpered, and I went back to sleep.

Mum said she had recorded the charts anyway, and she bought me in a tape and a new cassette recorder. She turned it on, and it was booming and distorted, and I could just hear the bass, boom, boom, boom, and feedback. Turn down that racket, I said, please turn it down, I can't stand it. She said it was as low as possible, and perhaps it would be better if she gave me her handwritten list.

The charts hadn't changed as much as my taste. Despite not having listened to music for so long, I knew that most pop was immature, banal, that a three-minute single couldn't really express feelings as eloquently as twenty or thirty-minute tracks. The *NME* and *Melody Maker* didn't call them songs any more, they called them tracks. Now some of the great tracks, the important ones, lasted a whole side or a whole album. And the albums were concept albums united by one theme. I think *NME* called it a leitmotif. The profound leitmotifs could only be expressed in albums, so the most mature groups had stopped releasing singles.

'It's crap isn't it, just total crap?' and Mum nodded though I'm sure she didn't grasp the significance of what I was talking about. 'All this music is just crap. You know Roy Wood, I'm so embarrassed I gave him my time because he's just, well let's be frank about it, and I know it was nice of him to give me all those autographs, but he's just crap isn't he? There's nothing to the music. OK so he played all his instruments and his face paint was clever or funny, but there was nothing *classical* about it, was there?'

She looked so hurt, and I bet she was thinking about her time in the Wizzard dressing room. She said she wasn't trying to be clever, but what music did I like now and how did I know I liked it? They had given me sedatives and some other new drugs after the operation and I couldn't help thinking they had made my mind less foggy. Actually, I was delirious. (I knew the word from a Yes track, 'Gates Of Delirium'.) There I was on the school podium, taking assembly. Andrew, John and Laurence were on the front row, as were Mark and Dave, who'd never been to my school. Dave was now portly and slack-cheeked, Mark was resting his head on a roof beam.

'Progressive rock is called progressive because it is just that. In the early days of rock 'n' roll and pop music, all we needed was three minutes to sing a simple ditty with simple words and a decent, hummable tune. But today rock is much more ambitious. It has progressed, and so have we. Some songs don't even have words and they all last a long time so the themes can build up, be sustained and transferred into our brains. Children, I would recommend you to burn your records by David Cassidy and the

Osmonds and Slade and Sweet and T-Rex, and possibly even the Beatles and Rolling Stones, although I accept they have all been important in the evolution of rock 'n' roll. I have been away from the classroom this last year exploring and discovering the rich and varied delights of progressive rock, also known as prog rock. For short. And in short I would recommend that you ask your parents to unleash you so you can make a trip down to Virgin records at the back of town one afternoon and go into one of their booths and fill your minds with progressive rock. Ask the young man with the long brown blow-dried hair tied behind his back with a couple of elastic bands to play you the latest releases of the groups Yes, Pink Floyd, Emerson Lake And Palmer, Deep Purple. But don't ask for hit singles because these groups don't release singles because they undermine the very progressiveness of progressive rock, also known as prog rock. When you have listened to these you may progress to Rick Wakeman and Mike Oldfield and Camel and Gong! Any questions? 'Yes, the tall one with his head in the beam?'

'What is this music about?'

'Well in the NME, *like Enemy, and the* Melody Maker, *the two serious music journals that I take, they discuss how these groups search for meaning in the universe and often all they find is madness. Groups like Yes explore the delirious vegetative monsters of mind and soul and sea. And that is partly why I am attracted to them. Is that clear? I know it's difficult, good. Uhm, yes, Andrew?'*

'What is the music like?'

'Oh, so rich and so complicated. They play long, beautiful guitar solos and often use instruments called moogs and synthesisers which sound like any number of classical instruments. Yes, the boy with the bag of prawns.'

'Do you really like the music?'

My head jolted. Perhaps I felt exposed by the question. I don't think Mum noticed I'd nodded off.

They didn't let me leave my bed for three days which was a relief even though it intensified the urine retention. I was bullish though. The Irish nurse was called Clare and she read me the *Beano* because my head was too sore. I asked her if she had steel sheets hammered down the front of her head.

'Clare, how much does your head weigh?'

'Dunno, love.'

'Clare, does the front of your head feel heavy?'

'No, I can't feel it, love, it's as if there's nothing there. Your head may be hurting because of the stitches,' she said, and I asked her what she meant.

'Here, feel this,' and she took my hand and pushed it along the back of my head. It felt rough and uneven as if someone had banged in a zig-zag of nails. I brushed against my head and just felt prickles. No hair, just prickles. I rushed in a dizzy curve to the bathroom mirror.

My beautiful hair. My beautiful black hair. My beautiful black greasy shiny hair. The hair that Dad's sister, Auntie Lena, had caressed as silk had gone. And the doctors, the bastard bastard doctors, had left me with two little flaps to cover my ears and nothing else but a gash of scar and stitches. They'd turned me into a Springer Spaniel.

I felt sick and looked again, and I searched under the two flaps of hair for the practical joke, the April fool, the hidden hair. Nothing. Nothing but a huge, bald throbbing dome. 'I want my hair, I want my hair back, Mummy where's my hair? Give it me back, bastards, I want my hair back.' I was screaming for my hair, my lovely fucking hair, and no one could hear, or no one was answering. And I wasn't sure if it was happening.

They said I fainted. That they went into the bathroom and I was lying on the floor, my bald dome cracked open next to a little pool of blood and vomit. A squad of doctors and nurses circled my bed. I couldn't hear their questions. 'Where did you put my hair? You never told me about my hair. Give it me back, you bastards.'

Dr Connolly came to see me and he pulled the plastic curtains round. I feared the worst, a suppository or catheter, but he said it was nothing like that, he wanted to speak to me privately, man to man. 'I'm sorry Simon, I'm really sorry,' he said. 'It was very thoughtless of us, horribly thoughtless. I had tried to prepare you for everything and just stupidly forgot about this. I'm so sorry. When you have an operation on your head, the doctors have to cut off your hair, shave it, actually, otherwise it can get in the way and cause infections. It was silly and insensitive of us to presume that you knew this, and I know what a shock it was when you went to the bathroom. All I can say, again, is how sorry I am.'

My hair was everything – my pop credibility, my calendar (I measured time by its growth), my dummy. And just razed like that. 'Do you know I'd been growing it so long that I would be able to stick it in my mouth and suck it like a pop star being interviewed. And what now that I'm bald?'

He told me my hair would grow back, even stronger. I didn't believe him, and what would I do when everybody called me baldy and slap-head and shiny bonce and Kojak. Couldn't they at least have had the grace to cut off all my hair? Dr Connolly said perhaps I should wear a hat for the next few months and that he had heard bobble hats were back in fashion. But I didn't want a hat because that would make my head even heavier and sweatier, I wanted a wig.

He smiled silently and sucked his lips.

'How long will it take me to get better now that you've done the operation? Will it be very soon?'

He said he hoped so, but he couldn't really say. 'After all, this was only an exploratory operation.' What's one of those, I asked, suspicious. He explained that it was an operation to try to find the disease but it wasn't an operation to cure it. He showed me an X-Ray and I could see the little tadpoles on my brain. 'You only have these if you've been poorly, and you obviously have been. We can't tell if this means the infection, the encephalitis, has gone or whether it is still there. I'm sorry.'

I can't remember any of the children from this stay, or any subsequent stay, in hospital. I'd turned away from kids so long ago they didn't register any more. Yet, contrary bastard, I still expected one of those big group cards – a four-foot tall blue teddy – from school for the op. Even they must realise how serious operations are. It didn't come, and I felt so bloody angry, and I couldn't help telling any sensible adult who would listen to me – you know, those bastards at school, couldn't even be bothered to send me an operation card, they've probably forgotten who I am or think I'm dead. Don't you think it's disgusting? Mum said there was probably a good reason. Perhaps they didn't know or perhaps they were so busy preparing for the eleven plus that they didn't have time.

Eleven plus? It used to be such an emotional phrase, the gateway to a future, to seniority, to exams and success and the adult world. Now, I felt nothing. Eleven plus? Who cares, so what? Poofters.

When I said sorry to Clare about being sick on her and told her why I had been, she smiled and giggled. She said it was very funny and asked what music I liked. She took me and my brutalist bald head in her arms. She told me I was like Kojak and that she'd buy me a lolly, and she rocked me, rocked me a little awhile, and I wasn't sure if I was awake or asleep.

I left hospital a couple of weeks later in my pyjamas and a woolly hat. A Manchester City hat. I'd even asked for the Manchester City hat. Reg had told me about Manchester City and it made no sense being a City fan. I hated Reg so why didn't I hate Manchester City? He had bought me a poster of City with Colin Bell and Francis Lee and Mike Summerbee hogging the front row, and I'd asked Mum to put it on my bedroom wall with a blue and white rosette. Even more contrary, Reg had told me that City were the Protestant and Jewish team in Manchester and United were Catholic, and I hated Judaism and Jewishness almost as much as I hated Reg.

Yet here I was in my City woolly hat and pyjamas leaving hospital.

The first thing we did when we got home was buy lots of magazines and I studied all the different haircuts. Women's magazines were good – *Cosmopolitan* and *Woman's Realm* often had features on men with nice haircuts, and *Shoot!* had all the footballers' haircuts. It took a week to decide. A feather cut like Brian Connolly was old fashioned now, short back and sides was a no-no, a Bobby Crush bob, a straight-down-the-road Kevin Keegan perm, a seaweed backwarmer like Rick Wakeman, a Freddie Mercury, a Colin Bell ear and shoulder muffler, a Bobby Charlton sweep over (the most practical), a Michael Jackson Afro. I really wanted a George Best long and straight and way past the shoulders, a George Best where you could flick the sides behind your ear or suck them as a comforter. But I couldn't have a George Best, I knew that. It was sacrilege, he was a Manchester United player. After much heart-searching and magazine stripping, I opted for the Jason King. Jason King, the London town detective dude. Jason King, Mr Cool striding down the streets twirling his 'tache and being wolf whistled at, and sidling over to his sports car with the open roof, and whizzing off in fourth. Jason King's hair could not have been more different from mine, except for the colour. It was thick and dry, and extravagantly curly.

Malcolm the hairdresser came round with his magazines. 'I want a Jason King, please Malcolm,' and he laughed because he presumed it was a joke. I asked why he was laughing, was he laughing at my bald head. How the fuck would he like it? No, of course not, he said, I've seen far too many slap-heads to laugh at them, but was I really sure about the Jason King?

'Do you know who Jason is?' I asked, dumbfounded. Of course, he knew. There was no cooler British detective than Jason. Malcolm said he had friends who would die to meet Jason, who had posters of him on their walls.

'If you insist I'll do it, but why don't we try a straight cut first, something a bit more you.' Patronising git. 'The trouble with a Jason King is that everyone will look at you and say Simon, why didn't you get a wig that was a bit more like your real hair, and Malcolm didn't do a very good job, did he?'

'That's the whole point, I don't want hair that looks like my real hair, I hate my real hair, it's digusting. And boring. My hair is the past. I want to be Jason King.' Malcolm told me how he'd done Auntie Lena only the other day and she'd said to him, you know Malcolm, I think little Simon's hair, even now and despite everything, is still as soft as silk.

I sat at my dressing table, with its hat trick of mirrors offering three different angles of me. Ever since the operation and the first trip to the bathroom I'd refused to look in the mirror. I still had the two runways of hair over my ears, and nothing else. My face was skeletal and yellow, my thick lips bloodless and chapped. My baldness made my ears and nose bigger. I looked like a chassid who'd seen the ghost of Jesus Christ.

Malcolm agreed to cover the mirrors with paper. He shaved my head with a number one, and the two patches fell to the floor and I already felt cleaner. For three hours, he primped and curled the wig. The comb flicking in and out, over and under to create the curls, and every so often he'd try it on me, and tell me how much better it would look if it was straight. He said I wasn't old enough to look like Jason King and I screamed for Mummy who came up to arbitrate. She took Malcolm out of the room for a minute and I know she told him that he was right, and it did look ridiculous, but just go with it, forget professional pride and she'd give him an extra quid to do a bad job. I wanted the hair to be so thick and curly that my face was invisible. 'Malcolm, do you think my shades will go well with the wig?'

It was late afternoon when Malcolm put down his scissors and comb and told me that was it, it was as near to finished as it would ever be. He apologised to Mum and refused to take any money. I told him it was beautiful, the best Jason King in Salford. Sharon walked in and giggled and walked out again holding her wrist to her mouth. Sod it. I didn't give a monkey's fuck what she or Mum or Dad or anyone else thought.

The wig wasn't that comfortable, to be honest. It was so thick and matted and sweaty, and it weighed more than any hat. So I didn't wear it often when alone. But I did enjoy rolling over to the mirror with wig and shades on and just imagining what life could be like. Early in the morning when everyone was asleep, that's when I did it.

The world changed when the others were asleep. I was terrified of light by day, and it made my eyes sting like crazy, but when they were asleep I would put on every light in the room – the main one (four individual lamps), the bedside lamp, the lamp in my sink, the light under the dressing table, even the light in my cupboard that used to give me a shock when I stuck my fingers in the socket. The room was fit for a memorial service, like one of those films where the stars go to heaven and are blinded by the white of God and the angels.

After the operation I began to listen to records again, properly. It wasn't that I felt better – nothing had changed, I was still the leaning tower of Pisa, my head still bruised with steel. And the hallucinations were getting worse – bugs in my head, pincered spiders grabbing at my brain, trapping the cells in their webs, and crunchy, black beetles scattered in an obstacle course. The internal builders bashed about in their steel toe caps, and when they squashed the beetles the crunch they made was agony.

Christmas came and went. And my eleventh birthday. Mum came up with presents and cards, which didn't mean much because they were all from grown relatives except for Andrew's. Nine cards. I'd got thirty-two the previous years when I'd only been in bed a couple of months: I remembered how I could never sleep the night before my birthday in the old days. It was getting dark in the afternoon, always raining. Rain was never seen, just a sound behind the woodpecker curtains

Sometimes I'd lie there in bed, thumb in mouth, thinking of the days we used to go to the clough in Prestwich and it would pour down and I'd take off my cagoole, sometimes even my jumper, and hold my head back as far as it would go and drink in the rain.

The operation had given me an abstract hope, which enabled me to listen to records again. I started with the old ones because I wanted to see if I could sing them like they sounded although I hadn't heard them. Sharon had mainly taught me Beatles songs, even 'Across The Universe' which was as complicated as it was wonderful. Some of the records I thought I loved I hated, some I did love and some that I wasn't too keen on were just fantastic. Mum had bought me 'Tie A Yellow Ribbon' just because it had been number one for so long that she thought it must be good. It was terrible, embarrassing, and I put it at the bottom of Sharon's collection. Sometimes I could sense Mum smiling at the door, watching me mull over the albums and trying them out.

Progressive rock was much more complicated than I had imagined. At first, I thought it was like the classical music that had bored me rigid at the Hallé, and you had to wait so bloody long for the chorus. I had to play it time and again till bits sank in, and it began to draw a picture inside your head. But before long I realised the rewards were far greater – this music explored new surfaces, and I was honoured that, even if it was from my bed, I was one of the people sharing this voyage of discovery to the Topographic oceans and the 'Dark Side Of The Moon' and the stairway to heaven, and Tarkus, wherever that may be.

The *NME* and *Melody Maker* journalists wrote long, learned essays on the meaning of darkness in 'Dark Side Of The

Moon' or the significance of the udder in the album cover art of Pink Floyd. I'm not saying I understood everything, but I did understand some of it, and I was proud of myself because I'd read that the average reader of these magazines were in their late teens or early twenties and some were at university.

There was a stack of records, outcasts, that had to go. Slade, the Sweet, T-Rex and Roy and Wizzard had no place in my life. Mum asked if I was sure, and wouldn't I regret it when I wanted to look back on my childhood and measure it out in record sleeves, and I wouldn't be able to because she'd sold them for tuppence.

Chapter Thirteen

I'd given up on the Jason King wig. I'd intended it for the outside world and as the outside world didn't exist it was pointless. My hair was growing back, slowly, lank as ever. I'd make regular trips, a few times a day, to the cupboard mirror to see if it covered my ears. So I decided to speed up the process. I took the scissors from Sharon's drawer and cut off an inch or so from the collar where it didn't matter. Then I lined up the hair on my dressing table, cut off a strip of sellotape, and stuck the hair to the edge of the sellotape and stuck the free edge of the sellotape to the rest of my hair beside my ears. Brilliant, I'd put on a couple of inches, just like that. But I was desperate to be able to suck my hair like a rock star. So I lopped off a few inches of fringe and sellotaped that to my extension. Victory is mine! Fuck you, razor-happy surgeons, my hair is back. I sat crosslegged on the floor in front of the mirror sucking my hair, thinking life's not that bad after all.

Hair was one of many obsessions that saw me through the days. You need obsessions to see you through the comatose days. And hair became my speciality.

Dr Connolly asked me about my plucking. He and Dick were the kindest doctors imaginable, but it would have been asking too much to hope he didn't have a plucking theory.

'Your mother told me you asked her to buy a pair of tweezers. A luxury pair, she said you said, the best money would buy. What d'you do with the tweezers, Simon? OK, I know what you do with the tweezers, but why d'you *think* you do it? You know it's perfectly normal for children as they grow into young men or young women to have body hair, it's certainly nothing to be ashamed of, or nothing to deny.' Dr Connolly didn't enjoy the conversation, I could tell. His eyes were more watery and distraught than ever.

I'd never thought about the plucking, I just enjoyed it, liked the feel of it. I liked it when it came out nice and easy from a juicy double-rooted hair and I even quite liked it when you had to yank it out. I liked the bald patches and little uprooted holes it left. After a session I would watch the holes fill in with newly formed flesh. After the pleasure, the regrets. By the next day I knew the plucked area would be raw and scabby and I always thought of Sharon saying never pluck pubic hair or hair around your nipples because it gives you cancer, and I felt I had enough on my plate without cancer.

My pubes and nipples were the two favourite areas, but I got pleasure from my thighs (a bitter twang as they come out), my eyebrows (nostalgia), my upper arms (twang), and my knee just around the map-of-Britain scar that marked the day I fell off my bike after the wasp sting.

Hair, pubic hair, fascinated me. I didn't understand it. Dr

Connolly and Mum and Sharon (I never told Dad, nor let him see) could talk all they wanted about how normal body hair was, but how could I be sure? I'd not seen another kid for years. One day I saw Sharon coming out of the bathroom with her ginger hair and I'd never seen it before. I chased her into her bedroom shouting Ginger! Ginger! Ginger! and I was grabbing her, trying to grab at her pubic hair. I just wanted to touch it, to rub her ginger splinters into my hand. I suppose she must have been scared, and she screamed, and Mum and Dad ran up, which made me scared. I just wanted to see, to feel, how her body was changing. I didn't mean any harm. 'What's the matter Sharon?' I said to her. 'I was only trying to touch your hair. It's new isn't it?'

She'd bought me a cassette of David Bowie's 'Hunky Dory'. I'd got all the new albums I wanted so I was catching up on the old ones I'd missed out on. Mum shouted up that Sharon had a surprise for me. And I said what, and she said, just a surprise, come and see. I must have been feeling better because I came down the stairs and they were in the living room listening to Ruby's stories. And when I took it out, I was so chuffed, I gave Sharon a kiss. And I sat there, crosslegged in my stinky old peekaboo pyjamas (holes courtesy of Mickey's teeth) just reading the sleeve notes and the lyrics as if trying to memorise songs I didn't even know the tune to. And the world almost felt right.

Sharon had just started her periods. There was a song on the record, 'Changes – Ch,ch,ch, Changes, turn and face the world'. Whenever I saw her I sang, 'P, P, P, Periods, turn and face the world, P, P, P, Periods . . .' I knew it was stupid and embarrassed her, but I couldn't help myself. I think I felt jealous.

But besides Sharon how did I know it was normal? And so what if it was? I wanted to tell all these people about the heaven – yes, heaven – when the one hair you were after just slides obediently into the tweezers or your nails and the ecstatic twinge when you tug it out. My very, very favourite area was the nipples. The hairs were nice and thick and whiskery and it didn't take an age to clear the forest. One by one I went round pruning until I was left with a stitched halo of pluckedness. The beauty was that they all came back, thicker and more whiskery sometimes with scabs and blood, and little lumpettes.

Chapter Fourteen

'How's about a holiday . . . in Spain . . . two weeks?'

She was trying it on, I could tell by the choke in her voice.

'What . . . D'you think I'm better then? One measly exploratory operation and everything's just dandy? Never been anything wrong with him that a decent walk and a punchbag won't cure. Fuck you.'

She was crying. I had a knack of making her cry these days. Part of it was her skin, the mystery allergy, the red contours round the neck and face. Part of it was me, and my capacity to upset her without even trying. I could make her cry at will. I remember we were sitting in Grandma's room, a few months after Gran had died, and Mum was going through her old clothes, and preparing for the arrival of the freezer that would replace Grandma in the spare room. And she was sitting on the bed, lost in the memories of an old photograph album. So many of the people looked identical. The men looked old before their time, even the young ones wore suits with watches attached to them and they didn't look one bit English. But I don't suppose they were. The ancient dead sepia women in pleated skirts that could house a family. And there were pictures of Grandma and Grandpa and Renee and Jane and her brother looking typically malevolent. Even on the photographs you could tell Grandpa was a joker, a handful, and that even he wished he wasn't such a joker. She was lost in the album and I put my arm round her and said, you're going to cry aren't you, and she did. It became a great game. Even though she hated it and told me not to, I think she also loved it because she knew it meant we understood each other.

'After all we've been through and after the operation, don't we deserve a little break? Don't be so selfish – there *are* others in the family beside you. Sharon and Dad haven't been away for more than two years, and if you really want to know we need a holiday, thank you very much.'

I told her to pack fourteen pairs of pyjamas. Didn't I want to take my spiv shoes, she asked. Of course, I wanted to take my spiv shoes even if it meant wearing them under my pyjamas. Mum had bought me the spiv shoes a few weeks ago – wet-look four-inch platforms and five-inch heels. She hated them, but how could I deny myself the opportunity of turning myself into an almost six footer? 'What about that stripy jumper, you know the one you can see all your ribs on?' She was humouring me, but I didn't care.

The trip to the airport was familiar. The cab, through town, on to south Manchester, past those houses with crucifix windows, every door the same but for the colours, passport control, duty free, Dad's fags, boarding and the hostesses with the big hair patting me on the head and telling me to have a good holiday.

Holidays smelt of petrol. All those times I'd been to the hospital I had never actually looked out of the window. Now all the old exciting smells were coming back, and as I looked out I couldn't believe how blue the sky was in winter, how cold it was outside rather than in my body, and how everything was still there only brighter and frostier than in my memory.

Strangeways tower was taller and more dick-like, Market Street stuffed with shoppers. The Arndale Centre, now complete, a massive shitty-brown toilet block on the sky line. And as we drove through town, all the time the smell of holiday came to me – cigarettes and petrol and cab leather and Old Spice and toilet water and the fresh air through the open window, and the woosh as Manchester passed by.

I shut my eyes and could still make out the outline of the city in my head, and every few seconds I'd open them to see if I'd guessed where we were up to. The world was brighter and colder, more tinselly, than I remembered, but not that different. On the flight I cuddled up to Mum, and Dad smoked into my face without realising it.

Spain was hot and blue and full of beaches. I didn't see any of them. There was no way Mum would be showing my tide mark to her friends when we returned home. I stayed in bed and read old music papers. Sharon won £4.80 on the bingo and she ran up and told me and we had a mini-celebration. I knew she'd win that night.

'You know what,' I said, 'I'm going to come down to

the pool and show you I'm still a good swimmer. Are there many kids about, are many of them English? I'm going to make new friends and we'll go to the beach and you can cover me up in sand, and we'll go searching for the man who sells gelati and coconuts. Do you remember the time we went to Bournemouth and we had coffee or chocolate eclairs every afternoon and we met those two kids who were a bit older than us? How they taught us to play strip poker and how Dad screamed at us when he walked in the room and both of us were naked except for your knickers? He was so shocked, remember? He didn't know what to say, he was speechless. He just stood there and ordered the other two out of the bleeding room with their clothes, and his hand seemed to get bigger and bigger, and he said he was going to teach us a lesson.'

I didn't go to the pool, or the beach, or make friends. I stayed in bed with ice packs on my head, complaining about the heat. And Sharon, who burnt at the sight of a holiday brochure, told me it wasn't even hot, barely warm.

I can't remember what I was doing in the lift. But I was there, and feeling quite cool. I had a pair of the most amazing flares – three buttons around the waist just like a waiter – over my pyjamas and my striped jumper and my spiv shoes. And my wig and shades. And I was on my way back to the bedroom when a family of four got in. They were British – their bag was full of Ambre Solaire and they were still peeling on the peak of their noses. The young boy, about my age, looked at me and nudged his mother and didn't say anything. But I was feeling self-conscious and went red, a new, unpleasant sensation, and then felt so angry that a little kid had made me go red. And his mother nudged his father who nudged the older son who must have been a couple of years older than me. They were Jewish, one of them wore a skull cap, and looked familiar, but I'd become so anti-Semitic I'd decided all Jews looked the same.

'Are you Simon?' asked the older boy, and the younger one chorused, quietly. It came back to me, both boys had gone to my school, the young one was in my year, my class. I didn't know what to say, I'd not spoken to any kids like that, kids I'd known, for so long. And I panicked.

'Simon who? I don't know anyone called Simon.' It was a stupid, hopeless lie and I was sweating without another word to say. It was obvious they knew who I was, and who would ever say they don't know anyone called Simon. What a fucking stupid answer. Brian's mother smiled at me and asked me if I was feeling better and would I be going back to school soon, and I looked at her as if she was mad, and her husband gently hushed her with his platform heel.

Back in the safety of the hotel room, my tears were hot and salty and angry and endless. Wasn't it bad enough being ill, without being scared of these people who didn't even mean anything to me? For a couple of days I lay there with the sheet over my head, and my temperature was raging. Dad said he thought two weeks was ambitious and that maybe we shouldn't have come at all. Mum stared at him, her mouth open in misery and incomprehension.

Sharon never liked holidays and seemed happy we were going home. Six days, not bad, she said, and promised she'd buy me David Bowie's 'Diamond Dogs' when we got home.

Chapter Fifteen

'Diamond Dogs' was for Mickey. We'd finally become friends. He didn't rip my pyjamas any more and I no longer pulled out his whiskers. A deal. Mum said when she went to collect him from the kennels he looked like he was mourning for his life. He was crumpled, his coat had lost its shine and his voice was hoarse. The woman who ran the kennels said she was so pleased our holiday hadn't worked out, that she'd never looked after such a depressed dog. 'Diamond Dogs' became Mickey's album, 'Rebel Rebel' the song I used to sing when Mum returned from the training class. Eventually he was chucked out of the class for unruly behaviour, being a bad influence.

David Bowie wasn't a progressive rocker, but it didn't matter. Like all the great pop stars he was into madness. I didn't understand the title 'Aladdin Sane' until I saw it in *Sounds* written as 'A Lad In Sane'. I thought about madness a lot. I had encephalitis which was an infection of the brain, so I was mad, yes? I knew everyone must think that, and I saw Andrew running round the school yard, shouting,

'Duh, he's mad! Duh, he's mad!' just like we used to Zig Heil.

I hid my wig under the spare bed, the one that Sharon used to sleep in. They knew they shouldn't mention it, pretend it didn't exist, and they were good about it. I don't know why I didn't just chuck it out. Well, I do actually. There was always that fear they'd scalp me again.

Three or four months had passed since the operation. The light through the woodpecker curtains was brighter, harsher, otherwise I wouldn't have known. It must have been spring again. I know Dr Connolly said that it was only an exploratory operation, but I still couldn't understand why I wasn't better. He said the operation had been a success, and then I was left to return to the nothingness of bed. Paracetomol and something for the streptococcus were the only pills I was taking, and the streptococcus was nowhere near as grand or serious as the encephalitis.

Dr Connolly said some illnesses have to go away of their own accord. I asked him what encephalitis actually was. 'Have you heard of meningitis?' he asked. 'Well, soldiers used to get it in the war sometimes because they'd been living too close to other soldiers in the barracks. Meningitis is an inflammation, an infection, of the outer layer of skin that protects the brain. Encephalitis is like that, but the inflammation is of the brain.'

'Mummy, my head is *killing me* . . . if the operation was successful, why aren't I better?'

'It was just an exploratory operation, Simon. An operation to find out what was wrong.'

'But they know now, so why aren't they making me better?'

She was staring into my bed sheets. Her voice was breaking up a little. 'The thing is Si, they know what it is . . . but they don't know how to treat it. They say there is no treatment.'

My temperature was up, but I felt cold and shivery and cheated. 'You told me, you always told me that doctors could make people better. You promised. What the fuck am I supposed to do now? What?' And I didn't want to speak to her or anyone any more. I wanted to be alone with my encephalitis, whatever it was. I turned away and put my head under my blanket.

'We've just got to wait till your body and head decide to get better.'

There was nothing rational about my hates any more, they'd become scattergun. I didn't dislike Roy Wood, I hated him now, despite his generosity. I hid the autograph book and badges in the drawer with Dad's Masonic pinny, and suddenly I decided I could no longer bear it at all, so I dragged it out of the drawer, and tore it into little pieces, and then I tore the little pieces into even tinier pieces and I threw them into the air.

Mum came in with mashed banana and asked me what the mess was on the floor. 'It's my Roy Wood and Wizzard autograph book . . . I'm sorry, I had to do it. It reminds me of the old days.'

The *NME* said there was a word for people like me,

people who loved lots of different music. Eclectic. They used the word eclectic so bloody often you couldn't help but remember it. Even though I had thrown out much of my collection, and was a progressive rock junkie, I felt my taste was bordering on the eclectic. There were plenty of records that didn't slip neatly into the prog rock niche, but there was one basic rule – each song had to have a guitar solo (except for Phily soul, like Harold Melvin, which never had solos). Simple. So my collection stretched to the Doobie Brothers, Golden Earring, late Beatles and Stones, (I took Mum's advice about not chucking them), 10 CC (until I heard that most of them were Jewish and raised in nearby Prestwich so I chucked them). And then there were the pop stars who weren't progressive but wore their make-up and sang their songs so stylishly that you had to love them – Bowie, Mott the Hoople, Cockney Rebel. Eclectic. If Andrew or Laurence or John knew the kind of music I was listening to, and all the grown-up music papers I read, they'd never believe it.

The more eclectic I became, the more obsessive. The more rigorous the standard. I'd never really had any problem with defining a guitar solo. The prog rockers were nothing but solos, while it was obvious enough that the thirty-five-second guitar blast in, say, 'Radar Love' or 'You Ain't Seen Nothin' Yet', were genuine solos.

Things went to pot when Mum bought home, on my instruction it has to be said, the Doobie Brothers' record 'Listen To The Music'. Only then did I realise how the guitar-solo rule could screw up life. A minute into the song, the lead guitar tweaked into what sounded as if it could be nothing but a solo, a distinguished one at that. Three seconds, five seconds, eight secs, nine secs and then nothing, just vocals and 'wo, wo woooh, listen to the music'.

It wasn't so much a matter of being cheated, it was the confusion. I listened again, five, eight, nine seconds, and 'wo, wo woooh, listen to the music'. And again, and again. For a week I couldn't listen to anything but 'Listen To The Music', and try to prove that it was a guitar solo.

And I didn't know, I just didn't fucking know, and when I was sitting down trying to have a wee or lying down sucking my thumb, or straining against the constipation, the one thing banging against the steel plate in my head was, is it a guitar solo, well is it? My brain became so crazed with guitar solos that it eased my headache, punctured a hole in my temple and eased the pressure. In the end I took a dart to the record and scratched the life out of it.

The more I listened to music, the more I complained about my head. It was the worry – if he can listen to this noise, there can't be much wrong with him. I turned up the volume after a couple of weeks as loud as it would go. It was an antidote, an alternative pressure, a balance. The headache of noise went to the back of my head, whereas the metal sheet, the buzzing and drilling, the workmen, were lodged at the front. And the headache of noise was weightless.

Dad came home with a portable black and white television and said it was for me.

'But I've not watched TV for more than a year, you know

the noise kills me. Thank you, nice thought, but another year maybe.'

'What I can't understand, Simon, is that you can listen to your music so loud, so what's the difference with a telly, and on the whole television is quieter. Remember in the old days, how you loved *Scooby Doo* and *Blue Peter* and *Magpie* and *Budgie*. Well, now you've got all the time in the world to watch what you want. Why don't you make use of it?'

There was no arguing, nothing rational I could counter with. He seemed to be challenging me.

'I'm *not* watching the television. Don't you *realise* what the pain is like? I'm living inside a fucking bubble, sometimes I can't even hear what you're saying, it's so loud. And sometimes I can't even hear the music, there's nothing but screeching and drilling and pounding and it's not fucking fair.' I tried to explain how the music worked as an antidote, but I didn't have the vocabulary and ended up a sniffing and snuffling wreck. He put his arm around me, and said, I know.

'What about if we moved the television in, and you don't need to turn it on, or you could have it on without the sound, and if you adjust the contrast you could even have it on with no picture *and* no sound? And maybe, just maybe, one day you'll want to watch . . . and maybe you won't. It's just an option.' He told me where the television had come from. The synagogue had a raffle, and he'd won – the first time he'd won anything in his life, he said, except for the coconuts he won at the fair every year. 'But I couldn't just take the television, could I? It wasn't right. They expected a little something for it.' I asked him how much. 'They said the telly would have cost £49.99 new, so . . . I gave them £45, and then I stuck in another tenner for good luck.'

But I did start watching the television, late at night when the house went to sleep. I watched late night/early morning television after a plucking session. I turned on without the sound so nobody would hear. It was one of those early seventies movies in which you'd see a flash of tit or the outline of a naked woman in the shower, all in the first five or ten minutes, sometimes even in the opening credits. I'd end up disappointed, but could always replay that five-second shower scene again and again in my head.

Soon enough I was outed as a late-night TV watcher, and the same old worries took over. Would they think I was getting better, would they send me back to school, would Reg come round aggressively pissed: 'I told you so, I told you so, you pair of bleddy malingerers.'

But after being outed, it was pointless to resist, and Mum was so delighted, who was I to deny her that shard of joy. So I became a telly addict and returned to the programmes that I'd not even watched when I was supposed to, four or five years ago. *Playschool*, *Andy Pandy*, *The Clangers*, *Camberwick Green*, *Trumpton*. The characters and presenters spoke so soothingly to me, especially the girls. So gentle and understanding. If they were doctors and if they came to see me they'd never force me back to school. They'd never say just because your weight is breaking six stone you're as good as better.

I was back on the music mags – *Melody Maker* had started a

new series, everything you needed to know about the moog synthesiser and veggie rock, which was a revelation. I tried drawing once or twice, but music had changed and so had my relationship with musicians. The glitter and make-up and gorgeous fuck-me corkscrew curls of Marc Bolan seemed shallow and narcissistic. There was an egalitarianism about the new music – Jon Anderson wasn't the only man in Yes, nor was Roger Waters in the Floyd, nor Keith Emerson in ELP. They were all part of a whole, neither more or less important than the others. And I liked it that way, it seemed fairer. But it meant they were harder to draw. It had to be the whole group or nothing, and after a few soiled attempts I gave up. But life, my nocturnal life, was fuller than it had been for a long time. I could spend hours, half the night, plucking, starting with my pubes and progressing to my nipples.

I kept the hairs in a matchbox and I would tip them out on to white paper and study the textures and shapes they made when bunched together. It was like that game Sharon once bought me where you shuffled magnetic iron filings around to define a man's blank face. I shaped my liberated pubes into a face and stuck them down on the paper with sellotape and locked it away in the drawer with Dad's Masonic pinny.

I also met Pam Ayres for the first time, although she tended to be on TV in the daytime. She didn't present children's television, but there was still something about her. Perhaps it was the big, kind mouth opening wider and wider. And the voice, so unusual to hear a country bumpkin on TV. And the poems which could have been written for you or me, and were just what they said they were. She wasn't trendy, would have looked ridiculous in spiv shoes, but somehow she wasn't a stiff either. Pam could get on with everybody, make everybody laugh over a cup of tea and morning scone. I watched her and wished that she, instead of Lesley Crowther, could do the early-morning ward rounds on Christmas Day and give all the kids in hospital their BBC Christmas presents.

[illegible], and [illegible] they went. She wanted [illegible] would have to [illegible] everyone [illegible] would [illegible] off [illegible] they would get on with [illegible] laugh over a cup of tea and nothing [illegible] I watched her and wished [illegible] Christmas [illegible] on the early morning [illegible] Christmas Eve and gave all the [illegible] Christmas [illegible].

Chapter Sixteen

I never made a conscious decision to be a poet.

I'd never even read poetry except for the Pam Ayres book Mum bought me. But I had read a lot of lyrics because that's all I could do when I wasn't listening to the music. And the words, the lyrics, were a kind of poetry. Often they rhymed or were set in blank verse.

The first poem I wrote was in felt-tip. I didn't know it was a poem. It was a doodle with words because pictures had become so much harder since rock had become progressive. I had a pad of drawing paper balanced on the edge of my bed at that 45-degree slant I'd always written at in my school days. Teachers used to say straighten your pad, Simon, how can you expect to write straight, at that angle, but I couldn't not write squiggly, I had to write at that nonsense angle.

The felt-tip pen was alien. It glided across the paper but sounded like a scouring pad battering a sheet of tin foil. It didn't matter, though. I'd forgotten the gentle push and swerve, the shapeliness of words. The first poems were derivative – find a Beatles title and invert it or exaggerate it. So 'Eight Days A Week' became 'Thirty Hours A Day', which I thought was rather clever. The early poems had choruses and lots of yeahs as in 'She Loves You, yeah yeah yeah'. And lots of ain'ts. They were pop poems, street poems. Mum used to ask where they came from, but she knew more than me. They were just locked inside, desperate to escape like a burp or a fart or a confession. Kids' poems, limericks, clumsy and trite, and bleeding with head pain and loneliness.

It's funny how happy you can make yourself being miserable. I'd seen *King Kong* before writing 'Happy's A Word Nobody Knows' and I loved the title because it was true to my head. The rhymes weren't perfect, no matter how many hours passed.

In a land never been heard of,
Happy is a word nobody knows,
They are always sad,
Cos they've got the gorilla nobody's had.

He eats children,
And pulls down houses,
And to add to that,
He makes the town look bad.

Happy's a word nobody knows.
They've never been shown
Any films or shows,
Cos in this land
Happy's a word nobody knows.

One day the gorilla fell in the sea,
And out of his skin came the lost prince,
And what a sight was he.

There were parties all over the town
And the word happy soon started to
spread around.

Mum asked what I was doing and I told her I'd written a poem. Can I have a look, she asked. I said no, but I wanted her to see. It was my work and I wanted her to see. Only one poem, but the pen felt right in my hand, and I knew I could develop like Pam Ayres had and become a serious professional poet, because I had so much time. I showed her and she told me how pleased she was.

'When was the last time you wrote anything?'

'About a year ago I wrote a letter to a music mag. I thought I'd forgotten at first, but it comes back really quickly.'

'Yes, it's like riding a bike,' she said, and it reminded me of my Chopper in the dining room.

'Mum, can you get me a proper pen and a pad of Basildon Bond paper with the paper with the rules so I can write straight, please?'

'Of course I will. You know, they always used to say at school that your writing was messy and squiffy, but it looks as if it's improved. Amazing what can happen if you don't do something for a year or so,' and she laughed and skipped out of the room. On the way out she rang the bell beside my bed – the bell I'd so often used to call her with – and giggled. I could hear her outside the room, talking. Talking to herself because I knew no one was in the house. 'My son the poet, meet my son the poet, *you know* the bedridden poet, the one who's not been to school for Christ knows how long. Yes, he's turned himself into a poet,' and she giggled again.

I wanted to write a poem about my head. The balloon, the loose screw, the light and drilling, the fact that I didn't belong to my body, that I was in the distance staring at it, even though I could feel its pain. I wanted to write poems about not being able to go out of my room, of my house, of Salford, of the country. Poems about the pain locked inside my head. Poems about darkness, about not knowing if you were dead or alive and how confusing that was. Poems about what it feels like when someone touches you, affectionately, with love, and it goes through you like Velcro, and you have to tell them to leave you alone. Poems about heat, body heat, the heat inside your head, being on fire, about the rush of an electric current through your head. Poems about being out of it. Poems about how difficult it is to be a poet, with countless distractions, people downstairs, toilets flushing, thermometers to be stuck in your mouth, mashed banana to be gulped, weight to be lost, doctors to be seen. How difficult it was to be a professional, a true professional, who could make every line or at least every other line rhyme and count.

Dad gave me his silver Cross pen. It wrote a smooth, rich blue, and came in a purple velvet case that clicked open and shut. The kind of pen a real poet would use. They bought me a stash of Basildon Bond, and I set to work. I moved out of bed on to the dressing table. So much more workman-like. At first I struggled over two or three poems a day, but by the end of the first week they were pouring out like a lather. I just moved my pen and they came, except for some of the trickier rhymes.

Mum said I was a boy possessed, and I suppose I was. After five hundred plus days of nothing, of near brain death, of floating in a double-visioned ether, here I was writing poems. An eleven-year-old poet. No longer was I excluded from the outside world because I was sick, it was my own choice. I'd exercised my own free will – sorry Andrew and John and Laurence and anyone else who knew me in my previous life, sorry lads, can't come out to play and Zig Heil in the playground, I'm a poet now.

Don't touch me
Or you'll get the shock of your life.
If you touch me,
You'll get a great fright.
And you'll see a burning light,
and the bulb inside the light would say
Look what I've found to eat, a nice, tasty piece of meat,

A brain!
But the kid touched me and instantly died.
She must have thought I had lied.
Don't touch me,
You know it's very dangerous,
It's very, very bad,
If it don't kill you, it'll drive you mad.
Don't touch me.
It's getting dark.
please turn on the light.
but please baby don't fight.

Cos if you touch me, you'll die,
So don't, please don't touch me,
Cos I ain't telling a lie.

I was working through most of the night and all the day. As soon as the others were asleep I had my light on, quick grab of telly maybe, just to see if Pam was on, though she never was late at night, then work and more work. For a break, I'd have a quick pluck or attempt a piss. My urine retention had eased slightly. I was becoming a master strategist. Rather than forcing my bladder through the eye of a needle, I put on my dressing gown and went into the garden, into the bushes. It was coming up to April and slightly less cold, and I stood there with Radio 1 and John Peel and some twenty-five minute Yes track, and just waited. Often within half an hour I'd have the piss done and dusted.

Eleven till three, work. Sleep till sevenish and then

straight up again. Barely bothered testing whether I was alive throughout the whole period. A quick grab of my pulse and that was it. Mum told me her friend Emma worked in publishing and asked would I like to see her. The thought terrified me. I'd not seen an outsider for ages. But I'd always liked Emma, she was bright and funny and read dirty books and wore high heels.

There was something tragic about Emma's life, Salford's Anna Karenina. When she died a few years ago, everyone talked about the smell, the terrible smell. A neighbour hadn't seen her for a while and he knocked and knocked and there was no answer, and the milk and post built up on the front step. And the house started to smell. After a few days he called the police and they beat the door down and she'd been lying there dead for three days, they said. All by herself, and no one even to miss her.

Emma came into my room in her high heels and her skirt that was by no means a mini but by no means full length, and her glasses balanced cleverly on the tip of her nose. She looked like one of those secretaries you'd find in a Carry On film – can you just take this down Emma, and she would and Kenneth Williams would guffaw. She was a few years older than Mum, which would probably take her to her fifties, and I found her attractive, sexy. She thought legs were there for showing off, bras were for firming up breasts and letting them walk six inches ahead of the rest of you, and lipstick should be spread liberally in passion red. It didn't matter that her hair was getting a little thin and sometimes through the curtain's sunshine she looked as if she had a bald spot.

She sat on the chair in the corner of my room, and I'd be in bed if I wasn't working or at the dressing table if I was, and she chatted to me about life. Life, desirable men, legendary romances, headaches and poetry. She primped herself and pretended she was my secretary. We made plans, Emma and I. Mum had said she was in publishing, but really she was a secretary, a posh secretary.

The lightning in my head was still flashing and my mouth was still a septic crater, but I was transformed. Not simply writing poetry, but a successful poet, with his own secretary.

'Emma, I'd like the latest book to be about twelve poems long. I think we should publish as soon as possible while I'm still hot. D'you think you'll be able to type them up over the weekend?'

'Well, we've got a wedding on Sunday and Matt has to get his pacemaker seen to.'

'Oh Emma, we'll never get this off the ground, will we? Well, what about Tuesday? Because we're going to have to send the book off to a publisher pretty soon, aren't we?'

'OK, with a bit of a spurt it should be do-able.'

'Thanks Emma, good girl.'

I don't know how she put up with me, the artist-cum-entrepreneur. But Emma and I understood each other. Not many people did understand me, and they were mainly women. I'd given up on most men, scoffers and sceptics and bastards. Two uncles refused to visit me in my bedroom because they thought I was a con merchant.

'Emma, I have a title for this book. *Beginnings*. What d'you think? It's one of the poems inside.'

'Perfect. It gives a real sense of what and who Simon John is. The beginning of your career as a poet and the beginning of you getting better,' and she smiled a long soft smile through her red putty lips. 'It's a lovely poem too, the pain and the hope really comes through.'

The name change. When I became a serious poet and Emma typed up my manuscripts I decided the time was right to change my name to something less severe, less of a mouthful, something more arty. I knew all about the likes of Cliff Richard and Cilla Black and Cary Grant. There had never been a great poet called Hattenstone, and I figured there never would be. So I turned my middle name into my last name.

Simon John. Simon John, the poet. The kind of name you could easily find alongside Roger McGough or Mike McGear of the Scaffold, the kind of name that could make it into the top ten with a poem-song like 'Lily The Pink'. I enjoyed my new image, felt at ease with Simon John. He wore big mosquito shades and twelve-inch bell-bottom flares and trousers with a four-button waistband, cheesecloth shirts and denim waistjackets, and he was so cool that all the teenyboppers and pre-teenyboppers would blush or look away or squeal as he passed. He wasn't aloof, he'd stop and chat to the fans, 'How's it going, gals, that's cool, yeh, you wanna be a poet, too, that's cool. *Far out*. Hey gals, if I can do it, from the sick bed, there's no reason you chicks can't from the outside world. Ride on. Far out. Nice meeting you, gals. Course you can have my home number gals, but don't phone after ten because Mum and Dad will be on their way to bed. *Coooooool*, far out. Cheers.' And I'd take a card from my cheesecloth shirt pocket, Letraseted, 'Simon John, Poet, Still Searching For Some Freedom', and sign it with an extravagant squiggle, 'Si. Love ya! Keep cool!! XXXX'.

Emma and I used to talk about our plans and dreams after a full day's work.

'What kind of cover d'you think we should have? A little picture of me inside an electric brain or a prison? Or just a picture of bars? Or rainbow colours? And who d'you think we should get to publish us? Can I leave that to you? I can't really be bothered with that side.' We decided there would be a head and shoulders photograph of me on the inside sleeve and a footnote thanking Emma and Mum without whom none of this would have been possible.

I did think my poems would be published. In fact, I considered them published once Emma had typed them up and indexed them, and I'd stapled and sellotaped them inside their folder. Mum and Emma told me there would be lots of interest from the outside world because people loved reading about what was going on inside other people's heads and I was still so young I could be a kind of prodigy. I went to sleep thinking of me the prodigy and what Andrew and John and Laurence would think that after all this time in the wilderness, in bed, in hospital, locked inside my own head, they saw me on television, only my name was now Simon John rather than Simon Hattenstone and I was being mobbed by a flock of girls.

I'm not saying all the poems were profound. We didn't want it that way. At eleven I had marketing nous, and it was something Emma and I would discuss in detail over the dressing-room table. If everything was miserable, the fans would feel down, so some of the poems were jaunty, love-struck banalities. Look, I'd say to myself, the Beatles wrote 'She Loves You' and 'Yellow Submarine' as well as 'Across The Universe' and 'Revolution', even Mike Oldfield released 'Froggie Went A-Courting' as well as 'Tubular Bells'.

I go for a motor ride
In the back I carry my bride
Over the hills I speed
Hoping the engine will not cease.
Like the wind I go.
Everyone is watching, I know.

Suddenly the car stops,
Everyone watches the wheels flop.
I get out and see what is wrong,
I see I'm missing a prong.
We put the car in a carriage
Off it goes to the garage.

The light poems were in the minority, though. They didn't

interest me, inspire me, and any poet has to go with his inspiration. And mine just happened to be pain.

Electric pain
Burning its way through your brain,
From the rain.
Does it hurt? Yeah!
Is it bad? Yeah!
Oh, it's driving me mad.
It's climbing your head
Whilst you're in bed,
And it's being fed
By you.
If you ain't feeling better,
And it's still that bad,
I can understand when you say
'It's driving you mad.'

I knew I would never be a song-writer even though I strummed my ukulele and used to strum the chorus of 'Stairway To Heaven' on my guitar till I smashed it to bits in a fit of despair. I was a poet and had to be satisfied with that. Pam Ayres couldn't have written 'Lucy In The Sky With Diamonds' or 'Dark Side Of The Moon', could she? But what I hoped was that the poems could be put to music when they were published. That's why there were so many yeahs in them – they could be turned into choruses by a skilled hand. Perhaps John Lennon, or Roger Waters of the Floyd, would pick them up. I chose those two because both of them were interested in exploring the inside of the head like me. Emma said it was called the psyche and I asked her if it was spelt 'Si. Key'. I knew it wasn't really, but when she showed me how it was spelt it made me laugh even more. Si. Key, si, key, psyche. It made perfect sense.

Emma's typing was fantastic. Not a single crossing out or handwritten word bubbling over a typing mistake. Once every couple of pages there was the faintest hint of Tippex but that was it. I loved the way she underlined every title and printed it in capital letters, and at the end of every poem ruled it off. So professional. I was very pleased with her, wouldn't have swapped her for anything or anyone. We used to talk about what we'd do with the money. It was no secret that, however close friends we were, she would get her due reward – maybe ten per cent, I'd not decided yet. I wondered whether I was being greedy, whether she should be on a bigger percentage, but you know I wrote the poems, I was the one crouched over my dressing table all day, fretting over the next couplet, I was the one who physically made the books, which wasn't easy.

How to Make Your Own Poetry Book

1) Write poems in best handwriting.
2) If you have an Emma type of friend or you happen to be able to type yourself, type them up. They look much smarter and more professional. Fans will be impressed.

3) If bedridden or bedroom ridden ask Mum to provide you with two ten-inch by six-inch pieces of cardboard and two full-size sheets of psychedelic wrapping paper. Make sure wrapping paper is abstract because images of Paddington Bear or suchlike give the wrong impression (as I found to my cost in my early days).

4) Apologise to Mum for forgetting stapler and scissors and ask her if she would please mind going out this minute because it is urgent and you have a deadline to meet.

5) Lay wrapping paper on solid base, cut wrapping paper in two and wrap paper around both pieces of cardboard and bind with sellotape. Take new sheet of wrapping paper, lay down wrapped cardboard pieces on sheet and sellotape them down parallel to each other with quarter-inch space and lots of spare wrapping paper at all sides.

6) Wrap sheet around two pieces of cardboard and sellotape down. Voilà, a book cover (hardback) with spine.

7) Draw up index and sellotape to left-hand side of book.

8) Staple poems together and sellotape stapled booklet into book, many times over so it doesn't flap free.

9) Turn over book to cover, type title and name of poet, cut into rectangular shape four and a half inches by two and a half, and stick on cover, making sure it is as straight as possible.

* * *

Not easy. But after the first couple of books Emma and I were becoming both quality printers and binders. She *did* believe we'd find a real publisher, but we were working on a ridiculously intense time scale. I knew my days were limited, but felt we'd made sufficient progress considering my career was only two weeks' old. The first book was handwritten and undeniably amateurish. By the time we published *Searching For Some Freedom*, the product, the whole project, exuded professionalism.

I'd been a poet a month by the time I was ready to send Emma the poems for *Beginning To Next*. She had also become my editor – she could spell much better than me, never confused her their and there and they're, which I did constantly. Would have been so embarrassing if we'd allowed those to slip through. She also made the odd suggestion, some of which I'd consider and reject (I was the artist after all), and some of which I'd agree were both sensible and helpful. I may have argued about it at the time, but of course she was right when I showed her 'Winter Night' and she suggested 'Branches swaying, horses mating', would read and rhyme better as 'Branches swaying, horses neighing'.

The poems were becoming darker, more painful and more of a release. Emma explained there was something called a Trepan when people, hippies normally, drilled a hole in their head and all their tensions and pains and miseries were released. Poetry was my Trepan. *Searching For Some Freedom*, the title of my next book, became my theme poem.

Mum and Emma were in the bedroom, and I'd stopped writing, exhausted, and returned to bed. My eyes were shut, blanking out the lightning which returned as soon as I stopped working.

They were talking quietly to each other.

'How are you feeling, Marjorie? You look so tired, you're desperate for a break, aren't you?'

'I suppose so, but how could I get away? How can I? And it's hardly the priority, is it? But you know I'm looking at these poems and the way he's talking to you, and his appetite, no not for food but for words and for work, and he reminds me of the old Simon and for the first time I feel hope, a bit of hope, that things could be OK.'

'Do you know he's written a poem called "Searching For Some Freedom"? Go on, read it. Have you ever seen anything more naked, from the heart. But he says it makes him feel better, Marjorie, he says it's as if every time he writes a poem more pressure escapes from the head, and he feels less likely to explode.'

'Yes I know. Thank you Emma, thank you. I don't know what we would have done without you. You should see his face when I say you're coming round in the afternoon, how it brightens up and then he remembers he shouldn't smile and he tries to look sombre and just says, well I suppose that's OK. But we both understand, don't we? You know what I find strange, that he's not moved in the outside world for eighteen months, he's never seen anyone, not his old friends, no children whatsoever, he's just stayed in bed, sucking his thumb and playing with cuddly toys and regressing, and suddenly not only does he have this unstoppable spurt of poetry, and not only is some of it achingly mature, but it's the way he thinks. So different from before he was ill. He used to be jealous of people with a newer or bigger car, every year he asked for a bigger birthday present, that kind of thing. Like so many children he was materialistic, not aggressively, but *things* were important to him. And now he's writing poems about poor little rich kids, and the curse of privilege, like, I don't know, a Robin Hood of poets . . .'

Surrounded by vast ugly walls,
Thinking of the rich
dining in huge noble halls.
I'm just searching for some freedom,
Somewhere to go.

I have got to stick around
miserable like the low
I'm put here innocent,
in a jail,
All I can do is look at the huge
Surrounding rail,
And search for some freedom
and something to do.

I'd been a poet for five weeks. Mum would call up

sometimes, and I'd refuse to answer because I was working. I was high, tripping with intensity, sleeping less and less, taking fewer and fewer breaks. Pouring over the words, sweat spotting the page, part temperature, part tension, part exhaustion.

'Searching For Some Freedom' had been a great success, at least in my terms. I thought the poems were good, Mum and Dad and Sharon and Emma said they were my strongest yet, a fair measure of what the fans would think. I was becoming more and more ambitious, and the next book was going to be a double album. Music and poetry always crossed over. It was 1974, and Yes and ELP and Deep Purple were going double-album mad, some bands even experimented with triple albums, and they were my inspiration. I'd released four albums in five weeks and my next was going to be my magnum opus, my 'Sergeant Pepper', my 'Dark Side Of The Moon', my 'Tales From Topographic Oceans'. 'Simon John: The Double Orange Album' it was going to be called. I had the wrapping paper, the cover, before the poems.

There was symmetry between my career and the Beatles. I wasn't being grand, I could just see it. The longer I worked, the more experimental I became. The deeper I trawled my mind, the more I freaked the fans. And the more intense the exploration, the more cynical I became about fame and the treadmill of work.

As the Beatles used druggy language and images, I also started to look for metaphors for my confusion. And I was never sure, nor did I care very much, whether the metaphors would be understandable to the fans, people who had never felt a steel plate through their head, or never had their brain invaded by creepy crawlies with spiked antennae and steel toe caps. What did it matter if they couldn't relate to an invasion by fingers in the dark? *I* knew where I was coming from.

I felt someone touch me,
As I was lying in bed,
And I was going very hot and red,
Cos it's fingers in the dark.

They were black and white,
And I had to put up a fight
To make them leave me alone.
Their fingers in the dark.

They're pushing me away from my bed,
Sticking one of their fingers in my head,
They're ghostly fingers in the dark
And it really ain't a lark.

Go away.
Drown yourself
In the Pacific Bay
Or even frighten the people
In the park
Just leave me alone,
You dirty fingers in the dark.

I was addicted to the work, the poetry. I couldn't leave it alone, but it was wearing me down. The sense of freedom was no longer there, the hole it had released in my head had been clogged up by the relentlessness of it all, by my own self-expectation. I was beginning to find fame cloying. I longed for the days of indolence, of thumb sucking and the uncomplicated agony of pain. It wasn't freedom from pain I wanted so much, it was freedom from my Victorian work ethic, freedom to go back to being a little boy, freedom to be infantile and hopelessly ill.

Thirty hours a day I work, or more
Thank God that ain't against the law.
Oh God I've gone wrong,
And I'm back to before.

Thirty hours a day I work or more
Last night I'd finished my book,
Now I'm on to another.
God ain't it a bore.

Thirty hours a day I work.
Or more.
I've never in my life known the word play.
And the few words I do know are 'come here
And bring the tray'.
Because I work a good thirty hours a day.

My temperature was on the rise again, and I was beginning

to smell because there was no time for baths. I told Mum that only once the 'Double Orange Album' was complete would I take a bath. It was unlucky, I said, I don't know why, I've got a feeling. I tried to grow a beard, but I had no facial hair yet.

My deadline was Monday morning. That's when I promised myself I'd hand over the manuscript to Emma and she'd rush off and type it all up, both albums, have them back to me for binding by Tuesday morning and the book would be out by Tuesday afternoon. Emma seemed to have gone quiet on me, but I didn't really have the time to ask her why. I suppose the tension was infectious.

As I'd been obsessed with guitar solos and album covers and plucking and music and pissing and shitting and loneliness, I was now obsessed with the concept of work, obsessed with not being able to stop. I wouldn't allow myself to sleep as my deadline closed in. By the sixth week, I was into the second part of the 'Double Orange' and Emma couldn't keep up with me. She told me I was too tired to work, that I was going to give myself a breakdown. 'Why don't you take a couple of days off?' she said.

'Are you crazy? D'you really think I can afford to take time off when the deadline's less than a week away and I've got a double album to put together? D'you know Emma, have you got the slightest idea, what the pressure feels like, knowing that the fans are waiting for you, and knowing that this album has got to be better than the last which had to be better than the last one before that which had to be better than the last one before that?' She was staring at me, and I think she was frightened of what she saw.

Tomorrow is another day,
And I hope it's better if I can say,
you don't need to do everything at once,
Cos tomorrow won't be
The end of the world.

You know you can't finish today.
Why don't you go and enjoy yourself?
Go to the sea-side and sit on the bay?
Cos tomorrow is another day.

But you don't take any notice.
You just sit and work
And drive yourself mad,
And for yourself that
Can be very bad.

Listen to me,
Tomorrow is another day
For you and for me,
So you don't have to work at all,
And certainly not as hard as can be.

I stayed up throughout Sunday night finishing off the last six or so poems and binding the double album in its psychedelic orange. My pyjamas were wringing wet, feverish wet, like they hadn't been for months. I thought of how the Beatles must have felt at the end of 'Pepper', or the Stones after 'Exile On Main Street'. I'd read in *Melody Maker* how a man called Captain Beefheart locked his band in a house for eight months while they recorded the album, and would only let one group member out a week to buy vegetables and essentials. I could relate to that, I felt I'd imposed that kind of regime on myself and Emma. I knew that the double album was more challenging and complicated than anything before, that I'd reached a new understanding about the demons inside my head and the nature of celebrity and the impulse to self-destruct. I also knew I'd never write another poem.

First thing Tuesday morning the door bell rang and it was Emma. She looked almost as wrecked as me as she came in with Mum. She'd wrapped the poems in a box with a ribbon and a Simon John sticker on top, and even though she tried to bounce into the room I knew it wasn't really there. The drive, the hunger had gone. The bald spot was definitely there and her hair seemed to have become more brittle over the weeks. She told me she thought it was my masterpiece, as she knew it was the end, and I felt terrible. Tired and weak and inflamed and fevered.

How do you begin to tell your closest friend, your colleague, your Man Friday, that it's over, the end, you're fired, we are no more? I didn't know where to start and I couldn't begin to speak through my tears. She sat on my bed, arms round my sticky pyjama collar, taking me through each page. It looked so beautiful and thick and she'd realised everything I had hoped for the 'Double Orange' album. The left-hand side was typed in blue, the right in red, the titles were bolder and fatter than before, and underlined in arty squiggle type.

Emma kept one hand round my collar and turned over the pages until we reached the end, which echoed the beginning.

Happy's a word nobody knows
They've never been shown
Any films or shows
Cos in this land
Happy's a word nobody knows.

'You know Emma, that's it. I won't ever write another poem. I'm sorry. I'm going to have to let you go.' I'd heard Dad say this about someone he sacked for fiddling the till. 'I'm sorry, I'm going to have to let you go.' And she held me tight. 'That's OK. We've been a good team, haven't we? We've done well. And you never know, in a few weeks' time Simon John may want to make a comeback when he's less tired and has had a break.'

I squeezed her hand and held on to it, comforting both of us. 'No, that's it. I'm sure. Will you be OK? D'you think you'll be able to find work?' Emma told me she still had her secretarial work and that, to be honest, she'd never thought this job was going to make her rich. 'I did it for love not money, you know Simon . . . But I still think we could send the book off to publishers. You just have to be persistent. I remember a friend whose husband worked for a publisher, and he always used to say it's not talent – though you have bags of talent – it's not talent that's important, he said, that makes your name, it's persistence, it's wanting to succeed, the pure desire of wanting to see your name on the book cover and the book cover in the shops. Desire, that's what it is.'

I told her I didn't have any of this desire left. I'd seen through the façade of fame, and I was too tired and hot and the demons in my head were banging away and stopping me think of anything else. 'I think they're trying to burrow their way out.' My hand was still held in hers and I said, it's been a beautiful friendship hasn't it, and I blushed because I never thought I'd say anything like that.

Chapter Seventeen

I think I took my retirement too seriously. Lay in bed, sweated, thumb sucked, and slept. After the double album I slept straight through for a couple of days. My language and behaviour regressed. I was back with the soft cuddly toys, only softer and cuddlier. I occasionally recited rhymes – Miss Polly had a dolly who was sick, sick, sick, so she called for the doctor quick, quick, quick. Mum sat by me on the bed and stroked my head and I'd say I want my Mummy, not knowing that I had her.

Uncle Tom, Mum's brother-in-law and comforter, visited and my head was a furnace, so heavy I couldn't turn my pillow. Tom, who was also a doctor, was by my side and I knew he was talking to me, and that his face was serious, but nothing made sense. I thought he'd lost his voice. He was standing there in a dog collar mouthing silent last rites and I presumed it must be time to say my goodbyes and thankyous. My head was delirious, tripping through its own internal movie. The bedroom filled up with row after row – old friends, relatives, teachers, doctors. Kneeling on the two front rows were the kids. Andrew was in the middle, clutching a leather football, captain of the team. He was reading a silent, distraught speech. On one side was Laurence, naked with T-Rex album in hand, and on the other was John, with a dove perched on each shoulder. Mark and Dave were laughing and waving cheerfully. Dave's face was covered in prawn shell, Mark was bent double because he couldn't fit in the room. He was a couple of foot taller than last time. The rows formed a banana-shape choir and began singing in white silence.

I didn't die. I just moved seamlessly into a dose of virulent pneumonia. It was more painful than anything before, but that must have been the effect of two big diseases for the price of one.

At first I felt I was losing my voice. Nothing more dramatic than a croak. Next day every syllable scraped away the area between chest and throat. A few hours later – it was as quick as that – every wheezy breath tore at my lungs.

Dad's car came up the drive, slowly, laboriously, as always, and I pictured his nose twisted into his eyes in concentration. He ran up to the bedroom, took one look at me, and said, Marjorie that's not a normal chest infection, call Dick and an ambulanceman. I'd never heard him so certain.

I was in the back of an ambulance staring through the tinted windows into the graphite night, a couple of nurses wrapping me in a blanket. 'Just a little jab in the botty, you'll just feel a little prick and then nothing.' Botty! I was eleven years old, and some fuckwit nurse was using the word botty.

If I'd been capable of putting together more than a crunchy wheeze I would have told her to fuck her 'botty'.

Hospital was a holiday. I was high on antibiotics, having a great time of it. Yes, the pain was bad, but how wonderful to have such a simple, non-ambiguous illness, an either/or. No argument, he's got pneumonia and this is what pneumonia looks like. I revelled in the comfort, I drank in the warmth, the sympathy, the fact that all the medical staff mollycoddled me even to the point of suggesting I wore my Auntie Lily neck collar in bed. For the first time, I didn't have to remind anyone my head was a building site, and my throat a septic gorge.

The six weeks went dreamily, the pain was blissful. You're ill, they give you pills, you begin to feel better, you recover. I couldn't believe that a disease could be so easy. They parked a bedpan underneath and ran over whenever I wanted anything, they didn't force food down me, and the doctors passed every morning and filled in a predictable recovery chart. They gave me drugs, told me I could attend the hospital school/nursery when I was ready, allowed me to listen to my radio, and sticky the sheets with dessert nougats.

Sister Annie told me I was beginning to smell, not nastily, matter of fact, kindly. She said I could do with a bedbath, and I squealed that I'd managed to be ill for close on two years, much iller than this, without going anywhere near a bedbath. 'Well, Simon do you really want to stink so that all the kids in the ward hold their nose and go poo, sniff up, Simon's about,' and I could see she was smiling. 'A bedbath isnt that bad, you know. At least you don't have to do any of the work. Just lie back and think of England.'

A nurse, probably in her early fifties, walked up to the bed with one of those plastic privacy curtains. I'd seen her around but never spoken to her – not that I was the world's greatest conversationalist. 'Perhaps we should have a bedbath today,' she said ever so gently, wrapping the curtain round my bed. She said she was called Nurse Annie just like Sister Annie but she was only a nurse, and she squeezed a green sponge into her bucket. 'The water's nice and hot, just right, not too hot.' Her hair was short, a fat Afro, and curled off into a wiry grey by her ears. Her hands looked tired and lined, especially when she turned them palm way up, white way up.

'When d'you last have a bath, Simon? You could certainly do with one my love, if you don't mine me saying. You smell so sweet and dirty, so sweetly dirty,' she said.

'It's probably a few weeks back, before the pneumonia.'

'Well you just leave everything to me, darling, because I can see you're in no fit state to do the scrubbing you need.' She squeezed the sponge into the water again, and the bubbles were soaking through the pores.

'Can you take your clothes off for me, darling,' she whispered in her crinkly voice. I said I'll have a go, and after a minute or so fumbling with my pyjama top, she laughed and said, 'You don't even have the energy for that, do you, darling?' She slipped her hand under the sheets and opened a few buttons down my pyjama top. She pulled the sides apart, so my belly was exposed, and moved round to the bottom of the bed, chatting, chatting all the time.

'How long you been here, then?'

'Three weeks, I think, but do you ever lose track of time, Annie?'

'Oh yes, darling, all the time, all the time I lose track especially when I move from days to nights. All the time. When are you going back to school then? Three weeks, maybe . . . that's a long time to be away.' I giggled and told her three weeks was nothing, that I was almost up to the two-year mark. Actually, it was closer to eighteen months but two years sounded more impressive and I felt I deserved to cheat a bit.

'Two years? My love, you poor, poor thing. What d'you do with all that time? You've probably grown four or five inches, I'll bet, since you were first poorly. My Lord, what a long time.'

She peeked under the mattress and with one practised tug, pulled my pyjama bottoms off and had them hanging on the bedstead. Just because she was a nice woman, with a good line in chit-chat, didn't mean I wasn't angry or self-conscious. When was the last time someone had to bath me? When? *When?* Never. Her flannel worked its way around my tummy and my nipples and under my arms and around my neck, and she pulled it out of the bed and smiled at me gently and said, 'Darling, look at all that muck crying to come out,' and she gave an almighty squeeze and said, 'It's like the Niagra Falls, isn't it, Simon, the Niagra Falls. Watch this . . . you'll love this, darling,' and she lifted the sponge way above the bucket and squeezed again and it poured down just like the Niagra Falls, straight into the bucket.

She dropped the yellow flannel in the bucket and rinsed and squeezed in some liquid soap and squeezed again and told me she hoped it wasn't too hot, and I should just yelp if it burned in any way. And the flannel rubbed up and down my ankles and in to that little crevice on the inside of the kneecaps where it tickled a bit and up my thigh and just when it got near the top of my thigh, I urged it closer and closer to the top.

It swooped back down to my knees and the ankle crevice and I wanted to scream out but what about my bottom, Annie, and my dick, you've got to clean that, that's the dirtiest, smelliest bit. And I could feel myself getting hotter and flustered, and when she asked if it's too hot and if I like having baths and if I'm a clean boy at home, I swallowed and couldn't answer, so I turned on my belly.

The hot soaking rag was gently digging into my bottom and wrapped round her finger and cleaning my hole and sailing up and down my cheeks and in and out. And I want to turn round and hug this Annie woman who is older than Mum and hug her tighter than I ever hugged Mum, and I want her to tell me that she loves me and rub me everywhere and rub some Savlon on my dick and bandage it because it's going to explode. And I'm still on my tummy and I can feel her big black white hands pressing for space under my belly and I lift it up slightly so she can get there, and I'm worried that she'll shout at me if she finds my dick hard. She makes circles with the rag and soap and cleans my tight little balls and I can feel the soaking spongy flag of a flannel over my dick which seems to be holding it up and I'm thinking I don't want the flag, I want you Mummy, Grandma, Nurse, I want you, and she's got soap on her hands and she squeezes it gently and cleans up and down once and I bury myself into those squeezing hands as far as I'll go, and she makes a circle with her thumb and index finger and squeezes so gently and I stop and I can't feel my head. She takes the sponge and cleans the creamy soapy water away from my belly button and gives me a little kiss on my cheek and tells me I'm clean now.

That was the last bedbath. I hoped for and was terrified they'd give me another one, and sometimes I saw Annie weaving down the ward with her trolley and bucket and sponges, and she'd smile at me and ask me if I was a clean boy. But I was getting stronger, my chest was easing up, although the throat crater was deeper and redder than ever, with a yellow yolk at its hollow centre and a white penumbra circling it. Mum told me, and she was almost laughing, that a few of my uncles whom I'd not seen for years had asked how I was and should they come and see me. 'I told them no thank you, he's doing fine, and why d'you think he'd just want a visit now?' And she said they said, well pneumonia's a terrible illness isn't it, it's obvious the boy's poorly.

'D'you know what I wanted to say, Simon, and you'll enjoy this because I don't use this word. But I wanted to say, why don't you go fuck yourselves?' and she giggled.

'What did you say, Mum?'

'I wanted to tell them to go fuck themselves,' and

we were both giggling like schoolchildren, which took us back a bit.

I stayed in hospital for six weeks, and I was revelling in my normality. Not normal in that my head or brain was better, just normal in that I could have an illness – even if it was only one of many, and just another sign of my knackered immune system – and make a recovery. By the third week, I was packed off, in pyjamas, to the hospital school down the corridor. I say school, but it was a smallish room with children from four to sixteen. Most of them were short stays, and they'd work away at their books from school so they didn't fall behind. All of which was an irrelevance for me. Where did I fall behind from?

The teacher was in her mid-twenties, and called Pam. She didn't want me to call her Mrs Pam or Mrs Whatever, just Pam, which I thought was great. She said she sang in a group, a folk band not unlike Steeleye Span. I tried not to pull a face. Folk music just wasn't there, except for Dylan. Mind you, when I returned to the loneliness of the ward I couldn't stop thinking about it – how cool, being in a band, the singer, and gigging. And having a crowd clapping, saying More, Bravo, Cheers, Cool man, or whatever they said at gigs.

Pam asked me if I went to gigs and I went red. It was a recent thing, this embarrassment, and I hated it. Stupid and pointless and about things I didn't give a fuck about. 'Well I suppose that's a daft question,' she said thoughtfully. 'You having been tied to your bed for so long. You're hardly going to rush off and see the Floyd or whoever in your pyjamas, are you? You'd get pneumonia all over again.'

'The thing is,' I said, 'everyone says that, don't they? You'll get cold and you'll get pneumonia. D'you know I'd not really been out of the house for eighteen months, and through all that time, or almost all that time anyway, I had a temperature. And I still got pneumonia. So how d'you explain that one?'

'Dunno! I'm not a doctor, Si. Just a not very successful musician masquerading as a teacher, sorry.'

Pam asked me if I liked Paddington books and I said I used to, and I told her about my cuddly Paddington at home and the marmalade sandwich under his hat and how I'd read the books at the previous hospital school. The hospital school lasted all morning every weekday. I was given special privileges because I was the only long-termer. She let me re-establish the old routine and it turned out she was even more skilled with felt animals than me, and we built a Noah's Ark in felt.

I never spoke to any of the other kids. I wasn't aloof, I just couldn't think of anything to say. I didn't know what you were supposed to say to children. Their lives seemed so different.

When I returned home, Mum set up this deal with the hospital and the education authority. Their letters had been getting more frequent and aggressive. You would have thought they were holding me hostage from the tone. So it was agreed that I'd go to the hospital school, all the way to Pendlebury, every morning, and come home in the afternoons and get on with being ill.

It probably sounds immodest, but my felt animals were

outstanding. Pam said so. Roy Wood portrait painter, poet, pop guru and now felt-animal designer extraordinaire, I was becoming a bit of a renaissance boy. Sometimes after completing a really difficult Tyrannasaurus Rex (tricky lumpy skin) or frog with poppy-out eyes and super spindly legs like a rotting geranium, I'd look at them in wonder. I did this! Pam wasn't even cutting out the shapes for me any more.

By the end of the morning I was back home and exhausted by all the activity. I just wanted to lie on my bed. Occasionally Mickey would come upstairs and flap open the door with his paws and come and lie beside me. I'd suck my thumb, and he'd clean his paws, and I'd show him a record by the Bonzo Dog Doo-Dah Band but he wouldn't get the joke.

Mum kept asking whether I'd go for a walk with him to the park, but I couldn't. She must have known that I was in no state to. Fair's fair, I was going to the hospital school every day, despite my throat and head, she couldn't have it every way. She said the park was beautiful in summer, and Mickey had become best friends with a Welsh bitch called Daff. Daff lived with two sisters called Kath and Megan.

Mum said she wanted me to meet them because she knew we'd be friends. She'd never met anyone quite like them, she said, and sometimes she thought they may not even be real people, sometimes she thought they were saints, not in that loose way you say he's a saint or she's a saint, but real, divine saints.

The pneumonia had cleared, and everyone was ridiculously concerned for me. The doctors had gone diagnosis crazy. They'd even convinced themselves I had a black mark on my lung – TB, cancer, who knows? The test, under anaesthetic, proved negative. There was a stability in this new arrangement. I no longer thought I was going to die, and the drilling in my building site was easing slightly, but I could see no possibility of getting better. That for me was the ideal. I still had music and television and some grown-up friends and Mum and Dad and Sharon, so there was a point to life. But what would have really killed me was a full recovery, going back to school, being normal, one of the kids.

It was July 1974, and I had recovered my sense of smell. It was only when it came back that I was aware it had left me for the best part of two years. I'd forgotten what it felt like to wake up to roses and honeysuckle and freshly mown grass, sunlight and blue skies shaped by fag-ash clouds, coffee and toast. I was even dressing myself in the morning for hospital school. My weight would up a few pounds, stabilise for weeks, then up a few pounds. I'd put on a couple of stone since the bantam-weight days, and I was a mammoth six and a quarter stone, only two and a bit stone less than when I started out.

But I wasn't worried, so long as they knew I was still ill, that I'd never go back to school, that it wasn't simply a matter of putting on a few pounds and being slightly less sallow than yesterday.

It became the summer of love. The summer of music, the

summer of Floyd. Dad was more relaxed with me. He felt more certain of himself and his relationship with me after he 'discovered' the pneumonia, well after insisting that I be rushed to the hospital with my stinking chest. I think it eased his guilt. He took some afternoons off work and came up to my room and lay on the other bed, the one that used to be Sharon's. Can you imagine it – Dad lying on a bed, taking his glasses off and listening to prog rock like an expert, a fan, a groupie! He still wore his suit of course, but so what if it got creased?

We listened and listened and listened some more. I don't even know if he realised everything was to do with death and madness and withdrawal and the loopy loo. His favourite, his absolute favourite, was Pink Floyd's 'Dark Side Of The Moon'. And mine. We'd lie there, him smoking his Senior Service, me sucking my thumb or my hair, blissed out, to 'Breathe' and 'Money' and 'Brain Damage' and 'The Great Gig In The Sky'. I'd turn the record over again and again, and then it was tea time. We always finished with 'The Great Gig In The Sky' and everything just floated away and upwards so softly that I knew if I did die – if something went wrong and I wasn't just permanently ill, and I actually died – things would be OK.

It wasn't just the theme of madness, it was also about money and greed, and big fat rich bastards that didn't know what to do with their lives. And I loved that. It reminded me of the people I'd known pre-illness, all the sad spoilt fucks that were probably crawling their way through grammar school at that very moment. The synths and moogs sounded like water on the brain and I closed my eyes and thought, does encephalitis look like 'Dark Side Of The Moon' sounds?

It became mine and Dad's album. He'd forget the name of the record, but always ask for it, you know the one that I love, the best group ever, now what are they called, Purple Floyd. 'You know, Simon,' he'd say, 'the Pink Floyd, they're the best aren't they, better than the bleddy Hallé Orchestra, real musicians. Marvellous.'

He talked about the time Mum and he went to a concert for me, 'that meshugee with the hair and face paint, but I tell you Simon, he was a clever man too, a good musician. And the bleddy noise was unbelievable, but you loved it, *loved it*. You'd say you had a headache and you felt dizzy and the light was piercing your brain, but you loved that music.'

We spoke about football and the pop charts and he pretended to understand both. We made plans to go and see some gigs at the Apollo. Once I asked him about Reg, did he still ever see him. And he began to clean his glasses unnecessarily. 'Yes, of course, I see him Si, he's my China . . . we just decided it's probably best for him not to come round while you're poorly.'

'You told me Reg would get me better, d'you remember Dad. You said he's always got people in our family better. Did you believe him when he said I wasn't ill?'

'No, Simon, of course not. But it was so complicated, he was my China and he'd never failed us as a doctor. Never.'

'But you knew about my headaches Dad, didn't you? You knew they were real? That they *are* real?'

* * *

'Dark Side Of The Moon' was written just for me. I understood it like I understood no album or person. I didn't even have to study the lyrics, I just knew. I knew that the prism on the front was about how people, everyone, interpreted their lives and their thoughts differently. I knew the title was about madness, the loony bin. I knew 'Time' was about the way it tricks us – slow, slow, unbelievably bloody slow, then it's all gone. I knew 'Great Gig In The Sky' was about a woman reaching peace through purgatory even though there were no words. And I knew 'Brain Damage' was about me.

The lunatic is in my head.
The lunatic is in my head.
You raise the blade
You make the change
You rearrange me till I'm sane.
You lock the door
And throw away the key
There's someone in my head
And it's not me.
And if the cloud bursts
Thunder in your ear

You shout and
no one seems to hear
And if the band you're in
starts playing different tunes
I'll see you on the dark side of the moon.

But I was already there on the dark side of the moon. I didn't understand how anyone could know me or my head or my encephalitis so well without meeting me. In the *NME* I read all about Syd Barrett, and realised the record was about him. Poor lonely, mad Syd .Barrett, the genius, the leader, who had found it too much and broke down and went to live with his Mum. Poor mad Syd who saw through money, who couldn't breathe in the polluted oxygen of fame, who lived on the dark side of the moon with me. I discovered that Syd had written the early hits like 'See Emily Play' before it had got to him, and although I never resented the four in the band now, it seemed so unfair that he'd gone mad and at the same time proved an inspiration for them. No wonder all the records seemed to be about Syd. Syd, the crazy diamond, was still shining even though he didn't know it. He was still their leader. And I knew if I ever met Syd Barrett we'd be best friends, and we wouldn't even have to say anything to each other.

Chapter Eighteen

They weren't happy with my progress. I wasn't so stupid as to tell them my long-term plan, but I suppose they saw for themselves. They saw that I had recovered from the pneumonia, put on a bit of weight, was listening to music. All pluses. They also saw that I was dysfunctional, alone, that I couldn't walk straight and they still heard me moaning with head pain. They certainly didn't want me permanently, mildly incapacitated. They wanted me better, and it just wasn't happening.

Dr Connolly ushered me into his colourless office and told me he'd heard great things about my felt animals, and how terrific it was that I'd managed to keep up the morning hospital school for three months. Then he spoiled it all by saying after virtually two years he thought I should be looking towards getting back to school.

'But I am at school, the hospital school, and I've read all the Paddington books and made more than forty fur animals, and Pam, the teacher, helped me make an ark for them.' I knew what he meant though.

He was talking to Mum, but he never lowered his voice, never hid it away from me. If I wanted to listen that was fine, no secrets. 'The longer I think about Simon, the more appalled I get, the angrier I get. I think we could have cleared up the encephalitis within a few months if we'd treated him properly.'

Or treated him at all, said Mum.

'I'm afraid your GP has got a lot to answer for. You could probably have him in front of the General Medical Council for negligence. Why the hell didn't he use his eyes and his textbooks? If it was me I'd have pumped him high on antibiotics. Literally, *high*. But he would have had to do that early for it to have had any chance of working.'

Mum said that she'd thought about it plenty of times, but it was more complicated than that, the relationship was too complex. Dr Connolly said there was a new drug that had been in development for five years and it was ready for use. 'It's up to you. I'm not pretending I can even so much as anticipate the results. Simon will be a guinea pig, and it will make him very very sick. It's an awful medicine, and because it's such early days they are not at a stage where they can make it more palatable. I don't suppose they expected to be using it so soon. It's entirely up to you. I don't know what the effect will be, just a hunch.'

She thought any of Dr Connolly's hunches were worth backing. They both looked at me, and I didn't know what to say. True, the thought of getting better wasn't worth contemplating, but on the other hand a permanently wrecked head and a body that caved in at the merest sniff of a virus wasn't a thrilling prospect. There didn't seem to be an option. What I really hoped was that the medicine would remove the steel plate and the lightning and throat crater, and leave me with just enough of a sore throat and headache – mild but permanent – to keep me away from the outside world.

Dr Connolly told us it had never been tried on a child before, never been used for encephalitis, although a form of it had been used in chemotherapy to treat cancer. I have to admit I did feel pretty special, especially when he told me the medicine would be driven down from the South of England in a Securicor van.

I can still make myself vomit at the thought of Marboran. It was a thick industrial yellow, much thicker than normal medicine. Pure chemical, and no attempt had been made to sweeten it. It's not as if anyone was going to nick it, but still it came in the Securicor van in a heavily bandaged box and inside the box was another layer of protective plastic popping paper. Each dose was in its own tiny plastic tub like children's paints. That's what it looked like – paint. The yellow was mustard yellow, like my Chopper bike. Although Mum and Dr Connolly had warned that it would make me sick I wasn't prepared. I heaved at the smell of it, and as soon as it went down my mouth I projectile vomited it back up.

Mum bribed me with the Yes triple album before taking the medicine and told me how I'd not balked at anything over the past two years, how nothing had frightened me. I still had some pathetic trace of pride. So we'd walk hand in hand to the bathroom and ready myself for the Marboran – it had to be in the bathroom so I could at least attempt to regurgitate into the sink. The course lasted a week, by which time I was vomiting day and night in anticipation. I asked Mum what was the point if I was just sicking it up anyway, and she said please, just try, Simon please.

The day I finished my course Dr Connolly advised another week. I puked. She put her arm round me and I pushed it away and told her to leave me alone because she went through me like Velcro.

The only thing to do was run away from home. I waited for her to go and get my papers from Cheetham Hill. As soon as I heard the car drive off, I put on my spiv shoes (minus socks) and a brown duffel coat over my pyjamas, wobbled down the stairs, opened the door – I was surprised I still knew how to open the door after so long – put up my hood and walked.

I'd got halfway down the street past the flats that had been knocked down and replaced by that massive modernist wooden block owned by the uncle of John's who was never seen. Fifty yards if that, and I was breathless. I imagined myself speeding down Bury New Road on my Chopper, my mustard-yellow Chopper, and I puked. I sat on the pavement, surrounded by my own sick, and sniffed the sweet and sour of recycled chemicals and sticky honeysuckle. The wooden house was opposite the park, and I could see my eight-year-old self on the grass playing football, my face brittle with determination.

A sign on the park read MAD MICK IS BANNED in capital letters. Mum had told me, but I hadn't believed it. We'd almost had a row. I said no one can be so stupid as to ban a dog, and she said well you can understand if someone crawled under the railings and ate your ducks, what else can they do. I'd got annoyed with her because I didn't think she understood my point: how can you ban a dog when the dog doesn't read. The park-keeper's house was battered, a couple of windows boarded up. Mum had told me how Jim the parkie had told her that the couple had moved away because of the violence – kids running up to the house, and throwing bricks through windows, petrol bombs through the door.

I wiped away some puke from my shoes and realised my shoes were my brown velvet slippers, and I felt so hopeless. I didn't know where I was going, didn't know how to get anywhere. I had no money, no direction, no dream beyond not taking any more medicine.

Paddington, Dick Whittington, The Owl and the Pussycat, and the boy who dug his way to Australia. They'd all made their own way in the world. My ambitions were limited to the end of the road and the old soldiers' home just thirty or so houses away. I'd packed a plastic carrier with essentials – 'Dark Side Of The Moon', 'Close To The Edge' and a luxury box of dessert nougat. The bag was weighing me down. I was sure someone had chucked in a couple of lead plates to thwart me, and I hauled it over my shoulder to rebalance myself. It took another forty minutes to reach the soldiers' home. I was limping and gasping and wondered if they'd take me in as one of their own.

The building was hidden by a brambled hedgerow where people encouraged their dogs to crap. I collapsed into the carpet of crap and bramble and wilting blossom and scanned the road. The row of houses were part of ancient history. They turned into the Italian beach from years ago, the miles and miles of anonymous beach. And me both lost and liberated. If only I had my Chopper I could get to the airport and stow away on a plane to Rimini.

But really I was just waiting. Waiting to be dragged home by Mum in handcuffs, cursing and kicking back home to the medicine and Reg standing at the door wearing a plastic face mask with false eyes and nose and moustache and a tub of yellow poison in his hand. And I knew I wasn't waiting for that at all, I was waiting for Mum to come and share the shit and bramble and blossom with me and put her head on my shoulder and say how sorry she was I had to go through this, and however much I kicked and cursed and told her I didn't want to be alive if this was living, she'd still love me.

I was shivering in the August heat, my eyes and nose fluey with tears I didn't want to wipe away. It may have been ten or twenty minutes or even less. She wasn't out of breath or terrified or any more distraught than I'd seen her dozens of times. I was livid at her certainty, livid that she knew she'd find me, and that she knew I couldn't run away to Rimini or to sea, but part of me just wanted to bury myself in her.

'I'm never, never fucking never going to have that medicine again because I'll fucking die, and then what will you do? Promise you'll tell Dr Connolly he can stuff his yellow poison up his skinny arse.'

She didn't say anything and I knew I'd take it for another week.

'D'you know all I need to do is think of it for a second and I can be sick.'

Of course, she knew. She'd seen it. 'Watch, I don't need to stick my thumb down my throat, I don't need to force a retch, you know like I used to. Ah! Bet you didn't know I used to do that, did you? Well you don't know everything then. No you fucking don't. And I don't care who tells me to mind my language because if they're so bothered and if they're so desperate to call the police and get me banged up, if they are, then they can fucking swallow a tub of it themselves.' The more I argued, the harder I swore, the more I knew that there would be one more week.

She did carry me home and put me to bed, and three hours later she woke me and carried me to the bathroom and said how sorry she was, but after this it would only be six more days. And I puked as she poured the tub into a spoon and it squirted up and down my nostrils.

I did start losing weight again. Hurrah! And Mum did go out and buy me a record every time I took a dose, which meant two albums a day for the week. Double hurrah!! And I did look more gaunt and transparent than for months. Triple hurrah!!! And I felt secure in the thought that if this makes me feel so bad, it can't possibly cure me.

At the end of the week I made Mum sell my Chopper and get rid of anything vaguely mustard-coloured. For months later I puked a couple of times a day at the memory of the Marboran.

But the summer of love did return. After a week's Marboran recuperation in bed, I was feeling more like my old self. Not my old old self, my original self, but the old self that was feeling slightly better than before, comfortably crap instead of let-me-die crap. I returned to the hospital school and the felt animals and made a terrific pink rhinoceros with glass eyes. I was becoming slightly stronger, and had enough energy to lie on top of my bed in the afternoon waggling my spiv shoes to the Floyd.

Mum was finding it increasingly difficult to shop for records, and she thought the time was right for me to go with her. I blew up at her, of course, and asked her how she could possibly think someone in my condition – *Mummy my head hurts!* – could go into a shop full of kids listening to loud music. I couldn't think of anything more exciting, though. She told me that the shop at the back of town was only tiny, but staffed by kids, just out of school or college, with fantastically long hair who let you listen to the records before buying them.

It really was as good as I'd imagined – pick out the cover you're interested in, toddle off into the booth, stick your headphones on and you're away. After a few weeks Mum said I could get the bus in by myself, and the 95 went up all the way to the record shop.

The summer of love part two was even better. Off to Virgin at one-ish, a couple of hours listening to new bands, then home to lie on the bed, back in pyjamas, deep in concentration. I never realised how sexy music could be. A group called Supertramp had a pair of tattoed tits on their cover so I bought it. And then there was Roxy Music . . . I whiled away whole afternoons studying the wet-water dresses and erect nipples on the cover of the album 'Stranded', shutting my eyes into fantasy. Were the nipples as brown as their promise? Did they taste like dummies or Rolos?

Every afternoon after hospital school I took myself to town on the 95 or 96 and sometimes the bus would come to a stop and resonate and I'd feel my dick going hard for no reason. I phoned up Virgin and HMV to see what time albums would be released and I'd get there twenty minutes early to make sure they didn't sell out, which they never did.

The pinnacle of masturbatory album covers came with Roxy Music's 'Country Life'. Two young women stared out of the foliage straight at me. Lipsticked and mascarad, in identical see-through panties, shaded with white daffodils and black pubes. The woman on the left had red nail polish and her open hand clutched her pubic area, her white bra tanned brown with nipple. The other woman had no bra on, her breasts – they looked more like breasts than tits, but I don't know why – cupped in her hands. When the house was empty I brought out the cover and studied it into a state of arousal. Why did the woman on the right have no bra on? Who had taken it off? Had Bryan Ferry been in the studio when the picture was taken and did he know the women? What did they do with the knickers when they had finished? Once I took the album cover on the bus with me to town, but the bus didn't resonate.

There was a time when I weighed myself a few times a day and now a week could pass before I thought about it. Even stranger, I knew I was putting on weight and didn't particularly care. It would have been great to stabilise at a ribby, semi-anorexic six and a half stone, but, well, who cares? Now I would admit in the open – well as open as it ever got – that there were certain foods I liked. Not didn't mind, liked. White spaghetti, cheese on toast with mustard, asparagus soup, chocolate cream eggs, Ruby's chocolate liqueurs, chocolate cigarettes again, Ruby's sugared almonds, dessert nougat of course. On Saturday Ruby came round after shopping in town and supplied us with more outrageous anecdotes and chocolate goodies. Best of all was cracking the head off a sherry chocolate liqueur, sucking out the sweetness and swirling the hollowed chocolate on the tip of my tongue till it melted.

Occasionally I'd even come down to eat with the family. My rules were rigid – no lights in the room except for a 40-watt bulb in a bedside lamp, I didn't have to sit at the table, didn't have to say anything, and didn't have to eat – and only then would I come.

Mum asked if I fancied making a chocolate cake and before I could stop myself I'd said ooh yes. Really, as enthusiastic as that. We whipped the butter and sugar and eggs, and threw in far more cocoa than we should have with the flour. I watched in front of the oven for forty minutes till the cake was ready. It rose perfectly and the extra cocoa made it just right.

Baking and cooking were just fantastic. Chocolate cake was no challenge, so I progressed to brandy snaps, chocolate eclairs with real choux pastry and Spotted Dick Pudding for Uncle Tom. I didn't like the Spotted Dick, but I loved its name. For a while, cooking became a career. Not an all-consuming one like poetry had been, just a regular job.

Casseroles, curries, spinach pancakes, spaghetti bolognaise, roast beef and Yorkshire pud – the little puds in individual cake tins – layer cakes with cream and strawberries inside, trifles drunk with sherry, soda bread, real bread, white wine from a Boots home-making kit, chopped liver for Fridays, chocolate rice crispy cakes like Laurence's mum used to make, fudge brownies, jam tarts, marmalade, potato and leek soup, carrot soup, rice pudding, bread and butter pudding, sticky toffee pecan pudding, fairy cakes with icing as dirty as Auntie Lily's, meringues, pavlovas . . . Mum bought me a chef's hat and an apron and I wouldn't let anyone in the kitchen while I was creating. No one except for Mickey, who would wander in and slink down by the pull-out stool or nap in his teeth-studded basket. He came in for the smell.

I'd resisted taking Mickey for walks to the park. Whereas town was anonymous, I knew no one and no one knew me, the park was a different prospect. I'd grown up in Broughton Park, played football and cricket there, fallen off the climbing frame, fed the ducks. Broughton Park was where the family would walk on the fast day Yom Kipur, and nod at the neighbours and friends, and gravely throw away their sins. Broughton Park was the old life.

'Simon, how on earth do you think you're going to meet up with all these people you were at school with at three in the afternoon on a Wednesday? They're at school. And if you did see Andrew or Laurence or John, you could either go up to them and say hi, where've you been all my life, or you could just ring up their schools and report them to their headmaster.'

I couldn't really argue with Mum. I'd forgotten the rules and hours of proper school. School had become an abstraction. Mickey was sitting on the window sill by the door, yowling for a walk. She gave me a handful of dog chocolate buttons in a polythene bag to bribe him back to the lead.

He pulled me all the way to the park, and I felt like an eskimo. Summer was drawing on, and the sun was low and warm, the flowers just beginning to wilt, nodding to the soil. Climbing frame, swings, field to the right where we played football, the pond with the bird house, seesaw, the greenhouses. Except for the trellis of sweetpeas running along the back of the houses, and the battered park-house, it all looked exactly the same, exactly the bloody same. Two years, seven hundred days on, and me and my head completely new, and there was the park unchanged. Look, there's me, as a nine-year-old running through the gate on a summer's morning, chasing the smells of all the flowers I couldn't name. I felt so excited, so bloody exhilarated. And Mickey was still on the lead and we ran and ran and outsprinted each other. And he was so excited that he was tripping up over his legs and his lead and my legs. We ran till we fell and wrestled each other over. And I was beginning to reclaim my world.

Chapter Nineteen

I didn't have a clue what Diane would look like. Mum just told me she was my friend. Which was doubly ridiculous. First, I didn't have any friends, I wasn't that kind of person. Second, I'd never met her, not even spoken to her at the time. Mum and Mickey used to go walking with Diane and Daff. I'd decided Diane would be head girl, very British, more proper than was proper. It never occurred to ask how old she was.

Mum and Diane would speak on the phone in the early evening before Dad got home from work, and she'd ask to have a word with me. Of course, I refused, so Mum relayed messages: Diane says she thinks you'd make a great team down the park; Diane asked me what do you prefer, Bar Six or Country Style? She says she's not that well up on football or music, but she's willing to learn; Diane says if you time it right you can get to the park when it's absolutely empty and still warm.

One day she phoned and everybody was out, and I don't know what made me answer.

'Hello, Simon. It's Diane. How are you? Mum says you seem to be feeling better?'

'No, I'm not. Not really. I'm still ill, you know. Just not quite as ill as before. But I could never go back to school.'

'I thought you went to school in the morning, Simon. That's what your mum told me.'

'Oh that, that's not school, that's the hospital school. But we don't do anything school-like at the hospital school. It's great, you should see it. All I do is read Paddington books for the second time round and make felt animals. If you showed me a picture of Daff I could probably make a felt animal of her. Is she big?'

'She's a little bit bigger than Mickey, and much skinnier. When are you going to come down and watch them play together? I've had dogs all my life, and I've never quite seen friends like them. They do everything together, everything. Run together, sniff the same dogs, kiss each other, pick over the same bones, go to the loo together. I think you'd love it.'

'Why's she called Daff?'

'It's just a name, Welsh, like Boyce. That's my surname. And Megan, my sister, that's a Welsh name too.'

'If I come to meet you and Daff how do I know what you'll look like?'

'Well, I don't think that's going to be much of a problem. For starters, there probably won't be anyone else in the park. And second, Mickey will sniff us out. But just to be safe, I could wear a rose in my lapel like they do in the movies.'

'Well I may come down tomorrow, but don't shout if I'm late or if I don't come. Because I'm not used to going out. And I may have a temperature or my head may be exploding.'

Diane said that was fine and if I wasn't there she'd be walking Daff round the park anyway.

Mum ended up going to meet Diane. She apologised and told her I wasn't feeling up to it. It's true I wasn't – when I got up I was clinging to the walls in old-fashioned dizziness – but I also thought it wasn't good form to turn up the first time of asking. OK, Diane and I had spoken on the phone, but she didn't *know* me, and if I was someone who could turn up at the park on the first time of asking, just like that, she may think that I'm better or there was nothing wrong with me in the first place. She could have been a spy sent by Andrew or Laurence or John or Reg or Barry. You have to be careful.

We set up the same arrangement for the next day. Again, she said it was all right if I didn't turn up. 'Does that mean you don't want me to turn up?' I sounded aggressive. 'No, Simon, of course I'd *prefer* you to be there, but I realise you can't predict how you'll be feeling, I know – well I don't know but I appreciate – what you've been and are going through.' It was such a perfect response – even the way she qualified the have been through with are going through – that I decided to turn up.

Diane was already in the park, polythene bag over her hand like a glove, wrapping up Daff's shit, sniffing the late-summer roses with Daff, just by the parkie's house.

I was only ten minutes late, but it was an important ten minutes. My greatest fear was being trapped there by myself, and seeing someone that I'd known pre-illness.

I saw Daff first. She had a skinny brown matted coat, so I couldn't tell if she was dirty, and deep-brown chocolate-egg eyes. I could see what Mickey saw in her. I'd never seen a dog smile before, but Daff smiled, almost laughed. She ran up to Mickey and tugged at him with her teeth. They looked at each other like lovers and ran off towards the climbing frame.

Diane bounded up behind Daff. She had her rose on, and was swaddled in a huge green anorak despite the summer. Underneath the anorak she wore a jumper and trousers so floppy and shapeless they almost weren't trousers.

'Hello Simon, I thought you'd come today.' For a second I was shocked, a bit disappointed. I realised why I'd asked Mum no questions about Diane, what she looked like, how old she was. In my head she had a Bet Lynch body, Marie Osmond face and she'd tell me we were made for each other in a girlie Swedish voice.

Diane was a few years older than Mum, fiftysomething I guess. Her hair was grey-blonde, her fringe hovered over her thick spectacles. Just the other day I'd been lying in bed, asking myself what was it about older women? Why were nearly all my friends older women? But this was taking it too far. There was old and ancient, and I couldn't contain myself.

'You're old, aren't you Diane? Even older than Mum?'

She opened her mouth in mock horror. 'I'm terribly

sorry, Simon, how old did you want me to be? Maybe you had a nice little picture in your head of me. Have I disappointed you?'

'Well, it's not that I want you to be different, I suppose I just hoped . . . you know, that you'd be young and pretty. Young and pretty, but still a few years older than me because I hate kids and if you were going to be my girlfriend you'd have to be older than a kid. And I hoped you'd have blonde long hair that you could stick in your mouth and suck like Suzi Quatro.'

'Mum told me you liked older women. Well . . . not this old, hey? Where have the dogs gone?' We couldn't see them. The park circled the pond. Mickey and Daff had run halfway round, crawled under the rails and were swimming back to us. The bob and weave of head and tail terrified me, and I shouted to Diane that he was going to drown, my Mick was going to drown and then what, then I'd be all alone.

'No, he won't. D'you realise how often I've seen Mickey and Daff do this? They're expert swimmers, could probably compete in next summer's Olympics.'

Diane laughed, and I told her there wasn't an Olympics next summer because it was only held once every four years and we'd had one last year. You have to test people out, don't you? Put them in their place. Diane told me I was a bit of a clever-clogs, which was great.

'Diane, are you into prog rock?'

'Sorry, love?'

'Prog rock? Progressive rock?'

'What's that then, Simon, can you get it from Blackpool?' and she opened her mouth high and startled and let her eyes roll into her specs as she so often did when she knew she'd been caught out.

'*Progressive rock?* Progressive rock is only the greatest form of music in the world. D'you know what eclectic means? No, well eclectic means that you have a really wide and varied taste in music, which I do. Because I've got records by loads of groups from Roxy Music to Hawkwind, and that isn't counting all the albums I got rid of by groups like Slade and Wizzard because I outgrew them. My very favourite music is progressive rock which is kind of like pop mixed with classical music. Loads of pop stars like David Cassidy or the Osmonds or even the Beatles in their early days, you may remember them, just sang about love. Well, prog rockers make concept albums that explore very complicated themes like madness, and how too much money and fame makes you crazy, and I understand about all this kind of stuff. I understand it all because I used to be a very successful poet till it drove me a bit doolally.'

'I see, so that's prog rock, is it. Electric, hey? Maybe you'll play me some one day. Can you dance to it?' I gave Diane a look so withering it took the smile out of her eyes.

'What kind of music d'you like, Diane? Bet you're into commercial crap, aren't you?'

'Well, I don't listen to very much music. Sometimes when I drive into work very early I listen to Radio 4 and the news, and sometimes Radio 2. Music . . . I used to like skiffle, but that's a long time ago, and you've probably not heard of it.'

'Not heard of it? You think I've not heard of skiffle? D'you realise for two years I've read every week, cover to cover, every single music magazine that comes out in Britain. And even some that just come out in America. I'm not saying skiffle is any good, but I can still tell you when Lonnie bloody Donegan was last in the charts and what his greatest hit was.'

'That's right Laurie Donegan. Sorry, Simon, Laurie Bloody Donegan. The way he rattled that guitar.'

'Lonnie bloody Donegan, actually. You're hopeless, Diane.' With her world-war voice and specs she could have been a Salvation Army officer. But if she had any hope of saving me she kept it to herself.

Diane was a devout Catholic. I couldn't understand it because whenever I thought of religion – Judaism first, but any religion – I always thought of those bossy fuckers who answered everything with 'Because'. Because that's the way it is, because God decided it should be, because God was testing us, because you can't, because it's written on tablets of stone. Because.

Diane and I agreed to meet at three in the afternoon the next day. Soon it was every day. Three p.m., the safe time, except for weekends.

'I hate God, Diane, I fucking hate him. Not that I think he exists. And anyway if he did perhaps he's Marilyn Monroe or a turkey giblet. I want to make a big banner and carry it around the park saying "God stinks, fuck off God."' I waited for a response, which didn't come.

'Well what d'you think, Diane, is God a cunt or what?'

'I don't like the word cunt.'

'Ok. Is God a fucker?'

'That's better.'

'Why is fucker God better than cunt God?'

'Because cunt is an ugly word. It's offensive and I've never understood why people decided it was the worst thing in the world to compare someone with a woman's vagina?'

'A woman's *what*?' It wasn't the first time Diane had surprised me. Why didn't she tell me off for fucking all over the shop, why didn't she threaten me with the police station? And how could she argue something so calm and complicated using those words? Sometimes Diane made me feel such a stiff.

'Well, you do know what cunt means, don't you?'

'I think so . . .'

'What then?'

Cheeky cow. That's my game. 'Well it means like fuck or bastard, it means someone's a bastard and you hate them . . . doesn't it?'

'Actually it means vagina. And, you know what a vagina is, don't you?' I must have been looking vulnerable and tearful and Diane would have never humiliated me, so she softened her voice. 'Like your penis, your willy, your prick, dick, your bobby dazzler, knob, doo-dah, whatever you call it, is your genitalia, so women have vaginas. And that's what a cunt is. Now I don't see why people should use the word vagina to abuse people with. Dick and prick and knob-head don't have such nasty connotations, so I think in the end it comes down to sexism.'

I couldn't believe it. Diane was saying knob and dick-head and prick. She knew all the words and was using them, and even though I didn't really understand what she was saying, or what sexism was, it made me think.

'What *do* you think of God then, Diane?'

'I like God. No, I don't like God, I love God. I have a good life, I have a sister I love and a father I love, and a job and a house. And Daffie, and you as a friend, so I feel lucky and I thank God for that.'

'But that's bollocks. If God was so fucking great, how could he have made me miss more than two years of school and how could he have allowed my head to be struck by lightning? How could he have given me such shite doctors? And I bet I know what you'll say. You'll say he's testing me, but I think that's bollocks because if he was a God with a heart, a nice God, and one that we should love, he'd make everything in the world good. And what about all the people in India who can't afford to eat, and the people locked up in Strangeways, and the couple in the park-house, and the people in Kersal stuck in those horrible high-rise flats with no windows? What's God done for them?'

Diane went quiet. She wasn't ignoring me, just thinking of an answer that she considered was right and explained things.

'I don't know, really. There are easy conventional answers that rabbis and priests give. They say that if there's no bad in the world how can you decide what good is because everyone and everything is the same. If you don't have to face hardship how can you tell what kind of person you are? And the rabbis and priests say this is just the first life, we're just babies on earth, and people who have hard lives and suffer a lot and are poor and are ill, have their good luck in the next life, in heaven. But it is difficult, Simon, I know. In the end maybe it's just a matter of believing or not believing. And I know it helps me to believe, it makes more sense of my life.'

Diane told me about her sister Andrea who was young and beautiful and a PE teacher when she died in her late twenties. 'Andrea had everything, and she just got ill and died. She had a man, a husband, a career. She was going to have children and she had the love of everyone who knew her, and she just died. Now I don't know how I would have coped, how I would have found a point in continuing and being happy, if I hadn't believed there was a reason for her being taken. D'you know what I mean, Simon? But I think it makes perfect sense for people not to believe. And to me it's the worst thing in the world, well one of them, to threaten or mock or scare people into believing in God. It's just as bad as ridiculing believers for their belief.'

I couldn't get the picture of Andrea out of my head. I thought God, if he or she existed, was a bigger bastard than ever, for allowing her to die, but Diane said things you remember, and the softer she spoke the greater the mark it left. When she said, 'It's just as bad as ridiculing believers for their belief', I could hardly hear her.

Diane took me to her house to meet her sister Megan, the cat and her dad, whose ancient mariner cheeks were hollow with age and stuffed with beard. He was older than the world. Diane told me he was ninety, and I couldn't believe it when he lifted himself from his chair and blanket and stretched out his liver-marked hand and said, I've heard all about you Simon, you're Diane's best friend, aren't you? I couldn't believe that he could remember, and I couldn't believe she considered me her best friend. Megan had arthritis. She was bent round her walking stick in an 'r' shape and her silver hair fell down her back like a fairy tale. Despite her back and face that told of a thousand daily struggles, she could have been a little girl, and we became close friends.

There were a couple of photographs of Andrea on the wall and she looked just as I had imagined. Her hair was black and strong, and she was much younger than Diane or Megan had ever been. Diane's dad showed me his crate of Guinness bottles and told me that's what kept him young. He said it gave him the energy to fight, and it also worked for children who were poorly. When Mum came to collect me, he took her to the side and whispered and she whispered back, and they hammed up their secrecy. On the way home she asked how I fancied becoming a Guinness drinker, a boozer. And we laughed.

Summer was turning into autumn, and I never knew I could talk so much, or listen so well. Sometimes I'd take a football into the park and kick my way round.

'What would you most like to do when you're completely better, Simon?' said Diane.

'I'm not going to get completely better. Never.'

'Why not? Surely you want to?'

'No, that would spoil everything. I'm not going back to

school either. You know my life is so busy that there would be no time for anything. If I was just like any other kid at school how would I be able to buy my records, and listen to them, and take Mick for walks, and meet you? What would happen if I decided to become a poet again, or an artist? I mean, what d'you think is more important, Diane, crappy old school or all this lot. And I have to go to the hospital for check-ups all the time, and what would happen if I got so dizzy that I couldn't stand up straight even if I was walking against the walls?'

'Maybe you've forgotten how much you loved school. You could meet your old friends and make new ones, and play in the football team.'

'I don't like playing in teams, I like playing in my bedroom. And the thing is I don't know my old friends any more. They never write to me. They're not interested in me, and I'm not interested in them. They go to those crappy grammar schools and probably spend all their life doing homework and going to the Hallé and being really swotty. And I'd never want to do that.'

'Does it upset you that you won't go to a grammar school? If you ask me, it's not important. I never went to a grammar school, and it didn't seem to make any difference.'

'Course it doesn't fucking upset me. I never wanted to anyway. I just didn't tell Mum and Dad. I just wanted to prove I could do the work, but I knew it was all crap. And I bet they're all really posh gits now. You know, if I met Andrew or Laurence or John now I'd probably just want to beat them up, the bastards.'

'But they've not hurt you, they've not done anything to you. Last time you saw them they were really good friends, so why wouldn't they be now? Don't you think they must have had an awful time waiting and waiting for you to get better and not knowing what had happened?'

'*They've* had an awful time? They've had an awful fucking time? Come on Diane, it didn't stop them taking their eleven plus and making new friends. D'you know they have never, not once, come to see me all this time?'

'But you told me you banned your friends from visiting.'

Every Friday we had our park feast. One week Diane would bring the chocolate, the next I would. Bar Six and Country Style most of the time. We'd sit on the bench and munch through it and every week she would say, 'You know what, Simon, I think it tastes even better than last week. Even better.'

We became famous in the park, friends with the people who worked there. Jim the head gardener knew me and Diane and Daff and Mick, and he used to joke to me about the time they banned Mick from the park and then realised it would never work because he couldn't read English. And Charlie used to kick about with me. Charlie was the park junior, eighteen or so. He was tanned and freckled like a baked potato. We talked about drink, even though I was only eleven years old, almost twelve. He'd tell me how he went down the Priory and saw United players there because it was just near the training ground and he said you wouldn't believe, you would *not* believe, how much some of them drank and how did they manage to play on that. Maybe, he said, that's why they were near the bottom of the first division. I sort of knew though, because there were lots of stories about George Best in the papers.

I couldn't compete with Charlie's stories, but I did tell him how every night after tea Mum lopped off the top of a bottle of Guinness and poured it into my pint pot, and even though it wasn't a whole pint it always reached the top because the brown stuff at the top was so thick and high, and even though I was only eleven years old I still drank it. Charlie told me the stuff at the top was the head, and that Guinness had a creamier head than any kind of beer.

Diane met a man and fell in love with him, and they got married and moved a few miles away to Eccles. I felt funny inside, and when Mum asked if I was jealous I got really angry with her. Every day Diane drove down to the park for three in that funny wooden Morris of hers, the kind lazy postmen used to have.

'Diane, why did you and Ron get married so quickly?'

'Because we're quite old, as you always told me, and we love each other.'

'Why d'you love him? He's not very handsome, is he?'

'Well he seems handsome to me, but that's because I think he's kind and generous and he wants to look after me. I never thought anyone would want to look after me, especially at my age, except Megan and Dad and Daffie.'

'D'you think Mickey and Daff are in love?'

'Well, I think they love each other, but I'm not so sure they're *in* love.'

Diane always made these subtle distinctions and if I asked her what she meant she'd always explain in simple words. 'I think they love each other like best friends or sisters and brothers. But if they were humans I'm not sure that they would be boyfriend and girlfriend or lovers.'

One afternoon a kid came up to me. He looked a year or two older and familiar, and I was terrified.

'Aren't you Simon Hattenstone? . . . Simon? . . . I said, aren't you Simon Hattenstone? Didn't you used to go to our school? You did, didn't you?'

I didn't know what to say. It was probably just a couple of seconds' silence, but it felt longer. 'No, my name's Simon John. I'm a poet . . . a retired poet actually.'

'Oh come off it, you're Simon Hattenstone. I remember you, you were at school. I knew your sister, she was my age, quite fancied her. And you got ill, didn't you? My mum said you went mad and were never seen again. That's right. You know, we were told you were dead, and this boy called Andrew gave a speech and went round the school collecting money for flowers because you were dead.'

Diane had her arm round me. She never normally put her arm round me. And I was determined he wouldn't see my tears, that they wouldn't come out.

'Well, you're him, aren't you?'

I broke free of Diane and smashed him in his glasses, which broke and fell to the ground. My fist was sore, and I was crying.

She walked me home, and I became calmer. We ate biscuits and Diane didn't ask me why I'd hit him like most grown-ups would have. She talked about Ron and told me that although he wasn't a Catholic he was religious. It was a strange, little-known religion, more like Judaism than Catholicism. When she moved into her new flat, she invited me round and told me she was changing her religion. Just like that. Goodbye Catholicism, hello World-Wide Church of God. She just sat there, on the arm of Ron's chair, with a cardigan arm draped round him, slurping her tea from the saucer as she always did.

'Isn't it funny, that now I'll be celebrating Passover and you Simon, even though you're Jewish, probably won't be.'

That's what I loved about Diane. So many people said how can you just switch clubs like that, and still believe in your new God? But Diane said faith was faith, and you had to choose the God and the faith that worked best for you. Because of her new circumstances, this religion now worked best for her, and she slurped some more tea out of the saucer and asked if I fancied another cup. Anyway, she said, she'd always felt jealous that we'd had such great festivals, and in the end everyone prays to the same God even if your God is Colin Bell or Tony Book, and she winked at me. How could she know all about Manchester City and just drop it into the conversation like that? But we had been best friends a long time.

Chapter Twenty

Mum said it wasn't a school in the real sense. They didn't have exams for starters. And, she said, you'll never guess what you can do after lunch – you can play football; all afternoon. I asked what the hours were for this non-school school and she started with a well, and as soon as she said well, I knew I was being conned. That it was a real school. I lashed out with my feet and my tears.

Turned out it was a nine till three job, pretty much like any school. And if she thought I was well enough to go to an all-day school she obviously thought I was better. Simple as that.

'Yes I think you're getting better Simon, slowly. But no, of course, I don't think you *are* better because if you were you'd be back at a normal school, and you wouldn't have to be dragged off to the doctors every week for check-ups and you wouldn't still be taking pills for your throat.'

I had felt so comfortable over the past few months, the summer of love – as much music as I could listen to, chronic, tolerable headaches and dizziness, sore throat, but nothing too painful. And here I was being turfed out of my illness on to the slag-heap of school. Bastards. For a couple of days I didn't eat.

I began to worry that Mum wasn't worried. 'Do you know I've not eaten anything for a couple of days? Maybe it's the encephalitis flaring up again? Perhaps I need a Complan drip?' And Mum smiled at me, which was just about the cruellest thing she could have done. She'd probably seen me sneak into the wine cupboard that wasn't a wine cupboard and nab some chocolate or into the biscuit tin that wasn't a biscuit tin for a handful of her meringues. Bastards. The truth is I was hungry, really hungry. Hardly a crime. I didn't have the energy to stop eating properly, to be anorexic. And how long would it have taken to lose sufficient weight to be diagnosed as even marginally sick – I was pushing seven and a half stone now. And the temperature had gone. Old faithful temperature had upped and walked out on me after two years. Bastard. I told Mum my head was killing and conjured up all the old images in one sustained go, and a few more for good luck. It was exploding, caving in, there was a steel sheet stuck down the middle, a beetle crawling down my meninges, I was trapped in a balloon, I was a Martian, my head didn't belong to me, my body didn't belong to me. Mum turned her cuddling arm towards me, and I winced loudly. 'Ooh, don't, it goes through me.' I suppose I overstated the case. It was true my head still did hurt and I was constantly aware of its weight, but it was a dull, comforting ache, not agony.

You couldn't miss the spikes. Angry spikes all along the

front. The school looked like a row of chalets, each class with its own veranda. We could have been in Switzerland.

Little Mr Walker was lost in his huge armchair. He pointed me towards the weedy chair, apologised for its smallness, and suggested Mum sat to the side, a referee. 'It will probably be difficult. You've been away from school for a long time haven't you? Months, no years?'

'See, I told you it was a proper fucking school.'

She looked embarrassed. Walker didn't blink.

'A lot of the children are quite rough and ready, on probation. They come from difficult families – fathers could be in prison, mothers too, in a couple of cases both of them. Some of the children are mentally handicapped, retarded, some have Down's Syndrome. In fact I think you can see a couple of our Down's Syndrome children out of the window, the one in the brown is Tommy and that's Dawn. They're in Mrs Singh's class, your class. So all in all I suppose what I'm saying is, don't worry if it takes a while to settle into a new school environment . . .'

'See, I told you it was a shagging school . . .'

'And to make matters more complicated Simon, you have to accept that it's not a school in the sense you ever knew a school. It will only be natural if you find it difficult, and if you have problems, remember the teachers are there for you, and I'm here as well. If something upsets you, someone upsets you, if you've got a bad headache, you just see your teacher or, if you prefer, come and see me.'

'Or sore throat . . . See Mum, I told you it was a proper school.' My voice was croaking with the betrayal, but I didn't want to cry, not now they'd chucked me back into the real world.

'There are only one or two Jewish children here and I think you may find a lot of the kids are . . . shall we say curious about your background, and the traditions.'

Thank fuck for that, at least not many Jews, I was thinking, and it almost came out. I could get away with a lot with Mum, but not that. I couldn't have got away with that.

The first day was a weeping day. Not loud or melodramatic, just quiet snuffling into a packet of pocket-sized tissues. Mrs Singh asked me what I liked to do and I said I liked making felt animals and told her about my legendary pink rhinoceros. She didn't know what I was on about. Not surprising, really. Schools and felt animals don't mix.

'Any books?'

'What d'you mean?'

'Any books you like to read in school, you know in lesson time? Can you read, Simon?'

Cheeky git. Could I read? Was she having me on? I nodded.

'Good. We have some book here, book for the children to read, English book.'

'I love Paddington. I've read all of them, nearly I think.'

'Good. We have Paddington book here. You will read Paddington book?'

The idea of being taught English by someone who couldn't speak it very well was reassuring. A couple of the kids told me she hadn't been here long, that she'd just got off the boat.

I asked what boat and a boy called Lee with a feathercut just like Brian Connolly said, 'You're a mong, you are, aren't you?' and he thumped me on the shoulder, playful but stinging.

'No I'm not a mong.'

'You are, you're a mong. You don't know what the boat is and you walk and talk like a mong, so you must be one.'

'I'm not a mong. Mongs can't talk.'

'Of course mongs can talk, you fucking A1 mong. You're not just a mong, you're a top fucking mong.'

I put my hand up, a reflex action from years ago.

'Mrs Singh, can I ask you a question, Mrs Singh?'

'Mongie's got a question for Paki Annie. Please Mrs Singh, oooh please, I've got a question, Mrs Paki Annie Singh.'

'Mrs Singh, mongs can't talk, can they?'

'Yes they can,' she said. 'Of course mong can talks. They not totally stupid you know, just different. D'you know what mong is?' She pointed out a couple of kids with fatty faces and globby eyes. They were the same ones that Mr Walker had said were Down's Syndrome children. I felt thick, really bloody thick, and blushed and babbled.

'But you see Mrs Singh, I thought mongs were mongrels not kids. You know, mongrel dogs. And mongrel dogs can't talk, can they?' I knew I should have just kept quiet. Even the mongs were laughing. Everyone was laughing and I tried to join in, but I couldn't.

Mongs, spastics, asthmatics and probos – kids on probation – were never going to make for a traditional classroom.

I remembered the old system of years one, two, three and four, all chronological and split into streams within that system. In this room, I seemed to be the youngest, but you could never really tell with the mongs and the spazzas. But I reckoned everyone was probably a year or two older than me.

One of the lads had starey eyes and a lolloping tongue just like the mongs, but he wasn't one. Stuart used to spend the day reading the bus timetables. He said his dad was a bus driver, but others said he didn't have a dad. He quoted timetables like times tables, and it wasn't boring, it was almost blank versishly poetic.

Nor was it school in the English, history, geography and maths way. Group teaching was a non-starter. Actually, teaching was a non-starter. The best hope was to dish out the books to the kids who could read and hope a few would look at them. The one group activity was book before home time, only it wasn't before home time. It was the last class before lunch and afternoon sport. That's why they called it an open-air school. Mrs Singh would shape us into a circle and ask for our requests.

'Have you got that book on George Best, Paki Annie?' asked Lee.

'Nah, that's bollocks, Paki Annie,' said Ned, 'and you know it is. What about a history of City, Manchester City, we are the lads who are playing to win, la la la.'

'Mrs Singh, what about Paddington?'

'Mrs Singh? Mrs Fucking Singh? Hark at the cunt. Look Simon, no disrespect, know what I mean, but the truth is

Paki Annie hates being called Mrs Singh, don't you Paki Annie. It hurts her, reminds her of home, know what I mean?'

I refused to talk on the way home. Mum knew I thought she'd betrayed me. '. . . Well the first day was always going to be tough wasn't it? . . . You'll get used to it, Simon . . . bet you like it before long. Remember how much you used to love school, couldn't tear you away at home time . . . I've got some dessert nougat and sherry liqueurs at home if you're interested . . . Ruby bought them for you as a special first-day treat.'

'I never fucking said it was tough. You said that, I didn't. And my head's killing me.' My banging, clattering head needed fresh air. I needed another hole in my head to relieve the pressure, and I couldn't tell if it was the encephalitis making a comeback, or the school.

'You never told me I'd be at a school with mongs and spazzas, did you Mum? I suppose you think I'm a mong too, just like the rest of the kids do. And why did you never tell me that mongs could speak, heh? Why?'

When we got home I forced myself to think of the Marboran, bullied myself into a puke. I could have reached the toilet or bathroom, but that was besides the point. I wanted to make the maximum mess possible in the most visible place, so I was sick over dinner, over the table, on to the floor. It splattered out to order, with a few chunks of undigested steak. True enough it wasn't orange, but I still felt pleased, vindicated.

'I suppose you'll still send me to school even though I've been sick.'

In the morning I covered a flannel in boiling water and pressed it to my face. When it cooled I reheated it, and did the same again. And again.

'Mum, I've got a temperature. Feel me, I'm so hot, and my head hurts. I want to go back to bed, OK?' I took my temperature and it was normal so I stuck the thermometer into Dad's teeth glass and filled it with boiling water and let it sit for a minute. The temperature bolted off the edge of possibility. I showed it to her, and she tried to shake it down, but it wouldn't budge. I think she realised, though she didn't let on.

'Look Simon, if you've got a temperature tonight I'll ask Dick to come round, OK?'

She left me just before the school as I had asked her to. I didn't want the kids to see her and I didn't want her to see the kids. Just a gut feeling. Through the morning I sat reading Paddington, the book covering my head and, much of the time, upside down. It didn't matter so long as it made me anonymous. Lee and Ned with their pop-star fringes spent most of the morning flicking rolled-up balls of paper at Paki Annie. I asked her if I could stay in the class at lunch with the mongs, and she said no because that was when they got their special help.

I'd not had a piss all morning. Tried twice, but the burn returned. At lunchtime I went and sat in the bog with my *NME* from home and tried to think of nothing to do with pissing. I read a story about the Bay City Rollers and it struck me that quite a few of the kids, the older ones, wore the same tartan just above the ankle trousers and there were a couple of lads who even had scarves dangling from their wrists. Fucking poofs. Bet they'd not even heard of 'Dark Side Of The Moon'. Nothing was coming, except for the burning dribble.

I went into the school yard and found an empty corner. A couple of lads I'd not seen before came up to me. Rollers fans by the look of things.

'All right, Jew boy?'

'D'you like it here at the old mongo school, you Yiddishe cunt?' They were older than me, two or three years older I think, and in between comments they looked back towards a group of kids for approval.

'Have you had your knob chopped then, Jew boy? Let's have a look,' and the one with the rolled-up jeans made as to grab for my dick, then withdrew and smiled. 'Only joking, only Jewking!'

A couple of other lads came over from the group. They were even bigger, and when they moved towards me the girls in the group tipped forward like boxers line dancing. They all wore leather coats to their ankles and short white socks and boots that weren't quite Doc Martens.

'Norman, d'you know that Jews live in mud huts and have loads of wives. The men that is, anyway, haahahahaha! That's why they have their knob done, me Dad told me, so they can shag better.'

'Is that true, Jew boy? Where's your mud hut?'

I'd not said a word. Don't cry, think of everything else,

think of the bedbath and Colin Bell and playing footy in your bedroom and the lyrics to 'Brain Damage', but don't fucking cry.

'He can't speak, can he?'

'Well, he's the one who reckons that mongs can't talk. And he could talk enough when he said that. You know our kid's a mong. He wasn't very fucking happy when I said to him, there's this Yiddishe cunt who's just come to school and he reckons mongs can't speak. D'you know what he said? He said, cos mongs can speak, right, and they can fucking punch like nobody's business if you get them angry enough, he said I'll batter the fuckin' cunt. And d'you know what I said, I said, don't worry our kid, stick your tongue back in, I'll fucking batter him for you.'

My lips were sticky with fear. 'I thought you were talking about mongrels, mongrel dogs, not mongs. It was just a mistake. I didn't know did I, but now I know, I know that mongs can talk, so tell your brother . . .'

'Tell my brother, are you telling me what I should tell our kid, are you now, are you fucking now, hey? You Yiddishe fucking cunt,' and his nose was touching my nose and I knew that when people did that it was followed by a head butt.

But Norman withdrew, and his voice calmed down. 'Sorry, that was rude of me, wasn't it? You know I'd forgotten you were a new boy, Jew boy. Hey, it rhymes that, d'you hear that everyone? New boy Jew boy, fuckin' A1, a bag of nuts, magic our Maurice.'

And the ring around us – it was a ring now – laughed

too quickly and said it was a bag of nuts. 'Hey lad, Jew boy what's your name?'

'Simon.'

'Simple Simon the Jew boy, the new boy – a bag of nuts. Look I'm sorry, we were only teasing cos you were new. Simon, and we were only joking about you being Jewish. I've not got nothing against kykes, me and me mam watched *Fiddler on the Roof* the other night, If I vas a rich man, didledidlediddlediddledey. Who d'you support?'

'City.'

'Who's your favourite player?'

'Colin Bell, followed by Dennis Tueart.'

'Hey cunty, I said your favourite, not two . . . only joking. Colin Bell's great, isn't he? Nearly all the lads at Rosewood are United fans, but I support City too. We'll drink a drink, a drink to Colin the king, the king, the king, he's the leader of our te-eam, he's the greatest inside forward that the world has ever seen. D'you know that one?' I nodded, even though I didn't. 'D'you stand on the Kippax? Kippax boys we are here, shag your women, drink your beer.' I nodded, even though I didn't.

'Well Simple Simon Pimon Jew boy new boy, you look as if you'll be a good lad. Welcome to Rosewood Open Air for Mongs.'

Norman stuck out his hand and I grabbed it and I knew I had to shake hard.

'Fuckin' hell mate, hard handshake, toughie, a bit of a Yiddishe toughie.' He pretended his fingers had been bent back by the force of my handshake. 'Hey Simon Pimon, simpleton, come here we want to show you something we think you'll like if you're a City fan. It's in the bogs and it's just A1, a bag of nuts, magic our Maurice. Come here, we want to show you something. It's amazing.' Norman and his mates marched me to the bogs.

There were two layers of circle now, the few girls on the outside, the lads on the protective inner ring. 'This one. Simon, Pimon. Let's just see if Lippy's finished. Lippy are you still in there?' I could hear the grunts and wet farts and splodges of a boy straining away. 'Won't be long now, Norm, almost done.'

'Good lad, you had that curry last night, didn't you, the Madras, the hot one, the arse blaster?'

'Can't you smell?'

'Now you mention it, Lippy, you did have a Madras? Or was it a Vindaloo? It was a fucking Vindaloo, wasn't it Lippy? Wasn't it? You did that for me, didn't you Lippy?'

'Uhhh, Uhhhhhh, splat, uhhhh. No, just the Madras. Wiping me arse now, be with you in a sec.'

A small boy with a scabby hair lip and the stink of diarrhoea walked out with an ugly grin. He nodded at me, as if he knew me. 'All right, Jew boy. This one's for you.'

Norman and Ned had me by the arm, not aggressively. Conspiratorial, but as if I was in on the conspiracy. The grip tightened and began to hurt. They pushed me into the bog, and one of the lads had grabbed my head from behind and was pushing it down. The bog lid was raised, and everything was happening so fast I couldn't see anything but a brown skin like yesterday's coffee. It was the smell – wet, squirty stinking cack and overpowering BO. There were more hands on my head and arms and I was being ducked and my hair was wet and I couldn't see for the shit in my eyes and I was choking. My head was under the water in the shit, and I was making bubbles to breathe. It was like at the swimming pool when you're under water and you swallow by mistake and the water jumps up your throat and out of your nose. Only it wasn't water, it was Lippy's shit. And all I was thinking was, don't cry, don't fucking cry, whatever you do, don't fucking bastard cry. And I couldn't cry anyway because my eyes and mouth were shut too hard, but I was going dizzy. Not dizzy like when I couldn't walk and had to hang on to the wall, but dizzy with confusion and dizzy at the thought that people were trying to kill me and dizzy at my impotence.

'Anyone got a fag?'

'Yeh, course Norman, here's a Woody.'

'Can you light it for me, Lee, I'm otherwise occupied,' Every time I gulped up more water and more shit, they tittered and closed the circle.

'Cheers Lee, the thing is, Simon Pimon, simpleton, Jewboy newboy, I can be ever so clumsy with fags at times. Don't know what it is, I get all nervy and they go all over the place.' The hot ash brushed my arms and the hairs sizzled. 'So-rreee, terribly sorry.'

I was going to pass out when they hauled my head out of the water. I spat out shit and water and piss and puke and you fucking bastards, but I don't think anyone could hear.

Norman said he was finished with his fag, didn't really like Woodies and had anyone got an ashtray handy. 'Oh lads, no worries. Silly cunty me. I've found one.' I screamed as the fag burnt through my wrist. 'Anyone got another fag, not a Woody. A decent one.'

'Sure Norm, how's about a JPS?'

'JPS, lovely, my fucking favourite. Hand it over. Oh no, I've just remembered, I'm allergic to JPS, silly cunty me. Anyone got an ashtray. No? Oh don't worry, just found one here.' The fag was stubbed out on my other wrist, and I screamed and swore but didn't cry. And as I saw the little black holes in my wrists and smelt the burning flesh, all I was thinking was don't cry, don't fucking cry.

I don't know if I passed out. But I was slumped over the cacky bog, and a teacher – not Paki Annie or Mr Walker – was hovering over me, offensively brusque, asking me if I shouldn't be out on the football pitch with the others or reading in the classroom. My head was drenched in shit and my hands were on fire, and this bastard was asking me if I should be out on the football pitch. I didn't even have the strength to tell him to fuck off.

I sat in the car and stared out of the window. Mum squirmed when she looked at me and my knotted hair and bloody face. I showed her the two black dimps in my wrists, and she was driving, looking straight ahead, making a dreadful job of not being distraught.

I locked my bedroom door and was going to plan my escape but fell asleep. When she banged on my door to wake me up next day, she asked whether she should come and speak to the headmaster, make an official complaint. Until then, I'd decided I would never spend another second at Rosewood Open Air for Mongs. Never. But when she said that, I knew she couldn't complain and that I had to go back and face the bastards. I hadn't cried, not at school anyway. The bastards had battered me and burnt me and made me their Guy Fawkes, but I hadn't cried and that had to count for something.

While for so many [illegible] other [illegible]
[illegible] danger [illegible]
[illegible] and [illegible] would [illegible] another [illegible]
[illegible] Orion [illegible] But when [illegible]
[illegible] complain and that I [illegible]
[illegible]
anyway [illegible] burnt me, and
[illegible]
[illegible] for something

Chapter Twenty-One

Paki Annie must have known because she looked at me and asked me if I was OK and did I want to stay in with the mongs at lunch. I went out and sat by the railings that bordered Gulliver Road. It was a plan of sorts. If they started anything, I'd vault the rails and run into the road.

For weeks I read Paddington, and stood by the rails in the afternoon just in case. I gave up on pissing at school, six hours containment was nothing. When I got home I took the music mags to the bog, and stole a couple of Dad's Senior Service, opened the window and concentrated on my hopeless smoke rings and watched the autumn leaves falling through the air like parachutists.

Phil and Steve tried to befriend me. They weren't mongs or spazzas, nor were they in gangs. They were wimps, and I felt more contempt for them than for Norman and his lads. They told me how they were only here because they were asthmatic and I wanted to smack them one although I didn't know why. My head was full of violence, I knew how to receive it, but I couldn't even make a proper fist for myself. Uncle Tom had once shown me how to make a fist so your thumb doesn't get broken when you punch, but I could never remember whether to lock your thumb into the knuckles or wrap them outside.

Once a week, Friday lunchtimes, Lippy was sent over to rough me up. It was a joke, and they enjoyed it. Lippy, pathetic, hair-lipped, pea-brained blubbery Lippy. They called him a mardarse, everyone knew he couldn't punch a hole in a balloon. Lippy would dance around me, hitting me on the shoulder and the cheek, not hard because he didn't know how to hit hard, but enough to sting. And when he went for my cheek he had to stand on his platform tiptoes. And the others would urge me on, go on hit the fucker, don't stand for that, you daft Jewish cunt, lamp the fucker, and I was petrified because I didn't know how and I didn't know if they'd just dive in if I did. I was the only person Lippy could bruise. He hated me and liked me for it, but I think the hate won out.

As I was going back into Paki Annie's, Ned spivved up to me, dead casual as if by accident. 'You OK, Jewboy? You know, the other week it was nothing personal like. A kind of joke really. Not very funny for you I suppose, but you know, no harm meant. You'll never guess what Norman said. He said, "That Yiddishe cunt, we gave him the best we could, the absolute fucking best of it, and the cunt still took it. Cunt." It's good that, isn't it? He was like, you know, impressed.'

What a dick-head, what a fucking dick-head, but I couldn't help warming to him, and I couldn't help being impressed that Norman was impressed. I knew it was the stupidest thing in the world, that they were mad, dangerous fuckwits, but part of me was saying, well they were only testing me out, you've got to test kids out, haven't you?

They put me in goal for the footy. It wasn't on the full-sized grass pitch, it was on gravel. The mongs and asthmatics and spazzas didn't play, the shittiest players went in goal, the second-shittiest players went in defence and so on. Unwritten rules that even the teachers agreed on. I'd never been in goal before, didn't have a clue what I was supposed to do on gravel, but I'd seen *Match of the Day*.

Lippy, shitty, hair-lipped Lippy, was a decent footballer. But not as good as Norman who played in his Roller Trousers, turned up even higher, and his red DMs, laced up to the knees. Norman let rip from outside the penalty area and the ball was going in the bottom corner and I flung myself across the goal just like Ray Clemence and Peter Shilton on *Match of the Day*, and I turned it round the post. But of course we weren't playing on grass. My cords were cut open at the knee, and there was blood running from my map-of-England scar. In the excitement it didn't hurt, it was almost calming, and I liked the way the blood soaked through the cords and turned the loose flap red.

They weren't used to seeing kids dive on gravel. I didn't realise there was an option. It didn't seem brave, just the only thing to do. There was one lad in the school bigger than Norman. Robert, Rob to his mates, and he was tall and broad and controlling like a Mafia leader. He was quieter than the other kids, but every word counted. Norman was Rob's man, and the rest of the school were Norman's men. Rob was even better at footy than Norman, not more skilful but stronger, and when he ran through from midfield, the space would open up like a bad centre parting because there would (or at least everyone thought there would) be repercussions if he was stopped. Again he ran through, and I came out to narrow the angle and he dummied me and ran round. I twisted myself back and dived on to the ball, and his knees clanged into my forehead. We were both hurt, but not prepared to show it. 'Fucking good save, you cheeky little cunt,' he said, and I swore he ruffled my hair.

Norman and Rob chose the teams and the goalies were chosen last. There were sixteen or seventeen of us, and I didn't bother listening to the selection because I knew my position.

'Oy, cloth ears Simon, you Yiddishe cunt, you're on Norman's side. Move your mongy arse.' Rob was talking to me, but I wasn't ready because they had only picked two players each. Fifth choice, I was the fifth fucking choice and a goalkeeper. I tried to look unphased, cool, and sidled over to Norman, but I couldn't help the thumbs-up. More saves, more blood, more scabs. Mum had her patching work cut out.

At break time Norman and Rob took over the gym. It was an invite-only party without invitations. You just knew if you were meant to be there, and suddenly I was. Twelve years old and in their group. Couldn't fight to save my life, and Norman would pat me on the head, ask me about my circumcised dick and mud hut, and recount some of my great saves to the line-dancing girls in their leather coats and monkey boots, his girlfriends. The girls would bring in their radios and tape recorders and play 'Shangalang!' and 'Bye Bye Baby!' and the lads would waggle their scarves from their wrists while pretending to ignore the music.

They talked about their plans for when they left school in summer. Norman would be sixteen, Rob seventeen, and they were mapping out all the time and space. Shagging, boozing, dole money and football, even if it was only in the amateur leagues, for Norman. I thought he could have been a pop star, not a progressive rock musician or anything like that, but a new-model Roller. Norman Phillips, pop star, footballer, likely lad who protects me and pats me on the head and tells me what good saves I've made, and when he's not snogging the girls in the gym puts me between the sticks and fires shots at me. Me and Norman. I suppose I had a crush on him, and I imagined us at weekends wandering through the park, big brother/little brother, scaring the kids, beating up a few cheeky fucks, practising our bounce-ups and swinging our tartan scarves. Norman Phillips. I'd not forgotten he was the bastard who burned me and dumped my head down a bowl of shit, but I'd justified it. He was testing my mettle, making sure I was up to the job. After all, it wasn't anyone who could be Norman's boy.

I no longer hated the open-air school for mongs, and I told Mum with pride how hard the lads were, how Norman was on probation for nicking clothes and beating up a copper, and how we were like a team, mates, and people left me alone because we were mates. She looked happy and appalled, and suggested that maybe the time was right to meet up with Andrew. He'd written to her – he'd given up on me – and told her that Manchester Grammar was exciting and challenging, but he still didn't like people sitting next to him in lessons because that was my place. Poor deluded fuck. I laughed when she suggested we meet up. Why? Why the fuck would I want to meet some stiff, wimp, posh-arsed bastard fuck who would rather be conjugating Latin verbs than out kicking the ball and kicking shit.

My record collection became outdated again. It's not that I actually went off prog rock, and in my heart I still thought 'Dark Side Of The Moon' was the greatest album ever, but it just wasn't practical being a prog rocker at school. All those boys from the Floyd and ELP and Yes were all posh boys, university boys, a world apart. Mum took me to the second-hand record shop in Bury and I twinged when I handed over all my albums and rebought a few Slade records and Rollers albums. Time had stood still in the outside world. I never really liked the Rollers, but you have to keep up with the times. I bought a tartan scarf.

Mr Smith became a friend. I can't remember what he taught – no one taught anything really. Maybe he taught football. He took me to my first match, just me and him, in the grand stand, watching Bell and Marsh and Tueart and Alan Oakes, who had never been booked in five hundred games, and Tommy Booth ('He's here, he's there, he's got no pubic hair, Tommy Booth, Tommy Booth'), and Chippy Joe Corrigan who was laughed at by the crowd because he ate too much fish and chips and was fat. I waited all afternoon for the *Match of the Day* commentary, but it never came. What a day, though. City beat Newcastle 5–1, Tueart scored a hat trick, Bell scored and looked fantastically nonchalant, a bit like Norman, when he scored, and Geoff Hammond, the right back who never scored, curled one into the top corner from thirty-five yards.

I was moved into Mr Randall's class with the lads who were preparing to leave school. A prefab past the football pitch with a television at the end of the room. We'd watch TV and talk about what we could do on the dole, and a couple of lads said they were going to get apprenticeships as joiners or go and work in Cussons soap factory, and that got a great roar until Mr Randall told us to shut up. He was a sherman tank of a man, skin like cheap wallpaper, near to his pension, football mad, and he swore more than us.

'Oy, you fucking arseholes, what's so funny about an apprenticeship? It's not bleedin' impossible you know, although I'm sure most of you would like to think it is. You cunty, why you smiling?' He loved the kids, all of them, and was convinced he could have made something of them, so he probably could have. If we'd been had up for kicking the Queen to death, Mr Randall would have been the first witness for the defence.

Not that I would have known how to kick her to death. One day a kid, Peter, younger and smaller than me, walked up to me when I was washing my hands, post football, in the bogs. 'All right, Jew boy?' He gobbed in my face and slapped my head against the sink. Norman and Lee and Ned and Rob said I had to beat him up. A matter of pride; if

I didn't kick the shit out of him, they'd kick the shit out of me. I had to fight tomorrow, and despite my Uncle Tom's best efforts I still didn't have a clue how to go about it.

It became the talk of the school. Simon – I was Simon now, even our Simon, our Si, our kid at times – was going to give Peter a good kicking in the corner of the football pitch, in the walled-off area away from the nets. Everyone would be there, and reports ran back and forth about how Peter wanted out, he was shitting bricks. But it couldn't be anything to do with me, it must have been the thought that if he won the fight he'd have to face Norman and his lads.

I couldn't tell Mum or Dad about it, and I couldn't sleep. When I shut my eyes I half-dreamed of a fight in which my fists were raw from punching air.

I was still considering running away when lunch arrived and Norman threw me on to his shoulders and chaired me into the ring. It felt good, great even, me on Norman's shoulders, the king, but of course it meant I had to win because he'd backed me. Peter walked into the ring, with two or three of his smaller friends. When he cracked my head against the sink and smacked me one, you know I'd never even spoken to him. I asked myself how? How? How, the bastard how? And before I knew it I was kicking and kicking and he was on the ground and I hadn't even had to use my fists. And his nose was bleeding, and I was enjoying it. The crowd were on my side and I felt their heat and I kicked his face and felt only mild revulsion. I wanted to try a punch, one, just one, a kind of therapy. So I hauled him up, and lamped him, and he flew back and another slug of blood shot out of his nose. I asked him if he'd had enough, and my heart was beating, and I was hoping he'd say no. Even though I knew it wasn't fair, I wanted him to say no so I could see another slug of blood.

I knew I had to say something, something to complete the victory. I was standing over him, my brown platforms resting on his chest, and I said, don't you ever, not ever, don't you ever fuck with me again, because I thought that's what Norman would have said.

Norman put me back on his shoulders and chaired me round the football pitch. He'd backed me and I'd turned up a winner. And I felt so bloody fucking proud. Lippy was there, and he'd never touch me again and if he did I'd just lamp him. If only Andrew and Laurence and John were there in the crowd. Looking up into the light and drizzle and I saw the three of them, their mouths open in admiration. No, Simon's not dead, he's a famous fighter now. Beat that kid in the first round, slugs of blood pouring from his nose, you should have seen it.

I would have never told Mum, but I was happy at Rosewood, in my element. Happy! Imagine that, me, *happy*! Reinventing myself musically was a small price to pay, and anyway what was so wrong in singing along to Shangalang! in the gym with Norman, the lads and the girls.

I became a story teller. They weren't used to stories, and I'd sit on the horse and talk about my illness and Mark with the dick to his knees and they'd all laugh, and I'd tell them that if they'd been there they wouldn't have found it funny, and Norman would say, get a bleeding sense of humour will you, Simon, lighten up. He'd ask me about the mud hut and say he never really believed in it. I told him my dad sold clothes, but never admitted he had a shop. Norman said I should try playing out of goal and I did, and he taught me how to do bounce-ups.

We went on nicking sprees locally and in town. They knew I wouldn't steal on the first trip next door to the grocers, so I kept a look out. But when we were sent to Mr Walker for a caning the lads said I'd not taken anything. I said I still wanted the cane – not guilt, solidarity – but Walker said I didn't deserve it, which pissed me off no end. We went on more dramatic nicking sprees in town – bus into town, running through Market Centre, up Market Street, and into Debenhams. We didn't care what we took, it was the principle of theft that mattered. I ended up with a handful of disgusting, tooth-pulling toffees. Dad's shop was next door and I was hyperventilating – the excitement of the raid, the fear that I'd be ordered to run through my dad's shop, pulling over the railings and taking anything we could grab before we were chased off. We didn't get caught, and we didn't stop off at Dad's and the year raced away.

It was summer, almost three years since the day I thought I had a bit of flu. My head really did feel better and I was even prepared to tell Mum. My throat was still a scarred penumbra, but the hole had sealed up. We watched the cricket in the prefab. Lillee and Thomson were bowling faster and faster, and the newly mown grass wafted in through the window. Mr Randall said this was his last attempt, his last-ditch effort, to convince us of the beauties of cricket, and the lads all jeered.

Mum wanted me to go to a normal school. However happy I was at Rosewood, it would have been daft to stay till I was sixteen. As the months rolled on I'd begun to pick up on sums which turned into maths and comprehension, and it was obvious I knew more than Norman and Rob who were ready for leaving. Mum told me how Mr Walker had said to her, one of the first things he'd said, 'Nothing good comes from staying at this school. The lads here never make anything of their lives, and believe me Mrs Hattenstone it hurts me to say so, it makes me wonder whether I've wasted my years. But it's true, nothing good comes of them.' The school medical officer was opposed to me moving. He said it was crazy, unfair on me because how could I catch up on three lost years in a normal school. She was a strong woman though, Mum. It's funny. She looked ten years older and her skin was full of those blotchy tell-tale stress marks, but she'd become more determined, more resilient. I think she had learnt that when she had a conviction she should stick with it.

Mr Randall turned down the volume, John Arlott and Richie Benaud moved their mouths in silence over the rain-ruined match, and he talked about the past and future. He said he'd never thought of himself as a teacher, and maybe he wasn't, but here he was, in his retirement year, having given his life to kids. 'Was it a good decision? Go on, you bastards, ask me, did I make the right decision?'

Norman asked him.

'I don't know, I don't bleeding know. That's my answer.'

We were talking honestly, maturely, like a group of adults. It was eerie, as if we'd been transported from Rosewood Open Air for Mongs to a more vulnerable, softer world. Lee said he was frightened that if he didn't get a job he'd become an alcoholic like his dad and brother and end up banged up. Rob said he thought he could get into the army, and the others were awed by his confidence, his ambition. Norman said he still wanted to be a footballer even though the trial with Oldham hadn't worked out, and Mr Randall said you'll have to make other plans though, son, other plans. Norman's head was buried in his Doc Martens and he said one of his brother's mates had asked him to be a bouncer down a club in town but he knew there was a lot of trouble there and he knew that the bouncers were just as often on the receiving end of it.

Mr Randall asked me what my plans were, and I suddenly felt so shy and young. It seemed so silly and small to say I was going back to a normal school, Kersal High, and my only hope was that I could fit in, just be normal. Mr Randall said that was brilliant and so brave and you never know, you may end up taking and passing exams when you're sixteen. The others also said they were really chuffed, that if they had their time over again they'd love to be at a normal comprehensive doing CSEs and trying for an apprenticeship, and for the first time at Rosewood Open

Air for Mongs I cried and I didn't care that they could all see me and hear me. And then Norman put his hand round my shoulders and asked me if I wanted a piece of bog paper to dry my eyes.

Epilogue

From a paper spoken by Marjorie Hattenstone to a medical conference in 1975

A month before his tenth birthday Simon became ill. He had always been an exceedingly normal, healthy lad – apart from children's ailments he was a hundred per cent fit.

We have another child, Sharon, two years older than Simon. They were always good friends and still are. During November 1972, Simon developed a virus infection – a temperature and a sore throat.

The doctor, a close friend of my husband, prescribed antibiotics, but they didn't help. The doctor then visited and prescribed a second course. By now Simon was becoming very lethargic, lying on his side in bed, with no desire to get up. I had never seen him like this, and became a little concerned. The doctor again visited. He said others got better on two courses of antibiotics and my best plan was to send Simon out for a good walk. It was a particularly rough and bitter week in December.

I asked if a consultant could see him and it was arranged. The paediatrician said there didn't look much the matter, but to be sure would have him tested in hospital the following day. There was one positive finding. His white cell count was high.

So again we started on antibiotics and although the white cell count began slowly to return to normal, Simon didn't. By now he was complaining of a constant headache and nausea. Apart from dry bread, he was eating nothing and he didn't move from his bed. His intermittent sleep was nightmarish.

With persuasion the consultant admitted Simon into hospital, but no secret was made that in his opinion, and our doctor's, the child was now swinging it. Simple tests were taken and were negative. Both the consultant and our doctor also said that I was a large part of the problem, that I was a neurotic mother who had projected an illness on to Simon. Thery offered me psychiatric help, and at one point I was so confused and disoriented by the whole thing I was probably close to accepting it. The funny thing is that I used to send Simon to school with colds and low-grade temperatures – I couldn't stand namby-pambying mothers.

When there was no sign of improvement a second time he entered hospital, and was sent to the psychiatrist, who said it was almost unheard of for a child of ten to have a depression, but nevertheless he was put on Tryptasel. This made him completely zombie-like. Apart from anti-depressants he was on no other drugs.

A third time he was admitted to that hospital and was given a lumbar puncture with negative results. He complained now of an unceasing headache, nausea, dizziness, and terrible difficulty in passing water. He was losing weight rapidly. At this stage it was decided to send him home.

We brought home a very sick boy. Apart from all else, we discovered that his bladder trouble was worse than anyone realised. It often took the best part of an hour of intense straining to pass water, and when he finally emerged from the toilet he could barely stand up from the effort. Incidentally, he had no idea that he was being observed. We phoned the hospital and were told to take him of the Tryptasel immediately.

The bladder trouble, however, lasted for months and months after this. It righted itself only gradually and slowly.

To add to Simon's wretchedness, he knew that not everyone believed him. I had already been told in no uncertain terms to stop fussing.

We didn't know where to turn or what to do. We decided to ask for a second opinion from a different hospital. After seeing him, this paediatrician said he felt we should immediately send for a neurologist or neurosurgeon.

Our GP called in a neurosurgeon (from the original hospital) and to quote him: 'There are more grounds here for further investigation than I was led to believe.' His opinion there and then was that the child had viral encephalitis.

It was now February. From now onwards for many months Simon did not come downstairs at all, nor was it possible to get him out of pyjamas. The GP shouted at him, and after each visit, Simon cried his heart out. By now he was regressing into infancy. He would stand at the top of the stairs, moaning, 'Mummy, I've got a headache,' and this was repeated all day long, every few minutes. No pain killer helped him. He couldn't bear the light, every noise went through him, he refused food, and he didn't want the radio or television. Essentially, he only wanted to lie in bed, sucking his thumb.

His voice, his facial expression, his bearing, had all altered completely. He said his head felt detached from his body, as though he was looking at everything through a plastic screen; that something was loose inside his head (in fact he said it was like a loose screw, and this was not because he was familiar with the expression); that he felt he was looking through the wrong end of a telescope; objects seemed like negatives on a photo; that his head was frozen; compared himself with the leaning tower of Pisa; said his walk to the toilet (his only walk) was zig-zagged; that his head was caving in.

Throughout all this, he was aware of himself. As though looking at himself from afar. He said he knew his mind had gone dull and simple. He only wanted baby toys, like little animals that jump with a pump, and these he would lethargically play with while he was lying in bed.

What, in my opinion, aggravated his misery was that he was keenly aware that certain people entering the house were hostile to him, or suspicious or doubting. Some even said in front of him that there was nothing the matter with him. After each of these occasions Simon was shattered.

His mood changed frequently. Sometimes he was ready to kill those who were obviously unsympathetic. He ripped his sheets in frustration. He no longer wanted physical contact with anyone, and even a touch would make him cringe.

Then he had a brain scan. Later he had an air encephalogram which was very painful, particularly as he still had the urinary problem, and had to sit on the toilet and literally sweat it out. This automatically increased the pain in his head. Right through the entire period he suffered from frequent and often long-lasting low-grade temperatures.

Many months after the onset of this illness, Simon went into hospital for a brain biopsy. The antibodies that were discovered convinced the surgeon that his original diagnosis was correct, although many of the previous tests had been negative. No one was sure how Simon contracted the encephalitis, but the most likely explanation seemed to be it was a consequence of a terrible leg infection he had a few months before he was nine when he'd fallen off his bike and a stone had been left undetected in his knee for weeks.

The surgeon called it chronic low-grade encephalitis and said encephalitis was unusual enough but chronic encephalitis was even more so. If it hadn't been low-grade, he said, Simon couldn't have survived it.

And many of us didn't expect him to survive. When they made the diagnosis, and Simon was regressing and regressing, I just presumed he would regress till he stopped being. I remember sitting downstairs – the whole house seemed so dark in those days – and I asked my brother-in-law, who was also a doctor, if he thought Simon would die, and he just nodded, silently. At one point I thought, the boy is suffering so much that maybe it would be better for him if he died.

I don't know if Simon ever thought about dying. I never mentioned it to him, he never to me. The more I thought about it, the more I would talk to him about what we would do when he got better. I think that terrified him as much as anything – the thought that he may get better. For months I went into him in the middle of the night or first thing in the morning when he was still asleep and checked to make sure the blanket was still moving up and down, and even then I wasn't sure he was still alive.

In summer it seemed worth taking a chance on a holiday. By now Simon looked not only disturbed, but also subnormal – a totally pathetic, broken figure. The second week of the holiday, again Simon developed a high temperature – all the old symptoms returned, headache, nausea, dizziness, hallucinations etc., and we brought him home ill as ever, and he returned to bed.

Matters began to improve again, very slowly. The only way to get him to eat was by feeding him. Every step forward was a struggle. One day we saw he had ventured downstairs and from the doorway was looking for a second at the television. He did this again on a few occasions, but would never actually enter the room and certainly would not sit with us. We thought it would be a good idea to get him a portable TV in his room, which we did, and the first time we saw him watching a programme was like a miracle.

He had still not been outside the gate except for visiting the hospital and for that abortive holiday. Next we bought him a dog and suddenly he found affection again. After many, many attempts we persuaded him to walk the dog out into the park across the road.

About this time Simon began a colossal outpouring of poetry. He had not written a word since the previous November and had never been interested in poetry. Suddenly he virtually could not stop. He sat and wrote all day long and halfway through each night as though possessed. I could not have stopped him and I didn't want to. After this frantic outpouring of strangely sensitive verse he lost all interest in his work.

The time had come by November 1973 to see the school medical officer since Simon had had no schooling for a year. It was agreed that he was only fit for a home tutor, but that we might eventually think in terms of a school for delicate children. (It seemed hard to envisage such progress at this point.) A tutor came for something like six times, then suddenly Simon developed pneumonia and he was rushed off to the hospital in his pyjamas, and so started a new phase.

By special request he was put in the ward of the consultant who had given us the second opinion months before, so his case history was already known. From the pneumonia he recovered reasonably quickly, was sent with the other children to the ward classroom and it was decided to combine medical with psychiatric treatment. But it was soon obvious that the psychotherapy was not helping him. After about six weeks it was the unanimous opinion that psychologically he had gone worse, not better, during his stay in hospital.

He worked satisfactorily in school, but talked to no one, then spent the rest of the day lying on his bed sucking his thumb. With the psychiatrist and the social worker he was totally uncooperative. It was decided that he should leave the hospital to be allowed to attend their medical ward school and the psychiatrist as an outpatient. During the vast part of this time he was still running a temperature.

Finally, the psychiatric department told me that they could no longer try to help Simon, as the emphasis of his illness was decidedly physical.

In May 1974, eighteen months from the onset of the illness, the paediatrician said that even if Simon was improving slowly, it was so desperately slow and distressing that he felt some direct anti-viral treatment would be justified.

A few weeks later he was put on a course of Marboran which made him indescribably sick, and heaven only knows how he was prepared to take the second lot, but he did. Am I correct in saying that no one will ever know if this really set him on the road to recovery or whether it was pure coincidence? But certainly, soon after, an improvement was observed and maintained.

The hospital schoolteacher and Simon had quite a nice rapport, but after a lot of thought it was decided to transfer him to an open-air school, which he began in the October. It was close on two years since he had attended a full-time school.

The beginnings there were traumatic to say the least. He looked the odd one out and so was a sitting target for the bigger boys to bully him mercilessly. The headmaster was always accessible, always understanding. One teacher in particular took a special interest in Simon and took him to his first football match. Thereby began the prime love of his life – football, and this interest was as therapeutic as anything at this stage. He learnt to hold his own, to play football with guts and courage. And at last he gained the respect of boys who were not interested in academic ability, but football prowess was the way to their hearts. After about six months Simon had made it. He was able to hold up his head again. The headmaster and I thought it quite feasible for him to return to normal school at the end of the year. The school medical officer opposed us, but we were prepared to take a chance.

In September 1975 Simon began at the local comprehensive. It was not easy but never was it traumatic. He felt he was no longer a *mong* (the dreadful name the children at the special school gave themselves), he began to take a pride in his appearance, in his work and in his very being. All the staff concerned knew a little of Simon's history and tried to ease his way. It paid off. He began to belong to the outside world again. With the help of good compassionate friends (mostly adults) every day brought an improvement.

Six months after joining the comprehensive Simon made a close friend and now two years later he and that boy are still as close. He is no longer different in any way from other boys. He has more than caught up with all the work he missed. The staff are as hopeful for his future as they were in the junior school before he became ill.

Those who helped our son, not necessarily with cleverness, but with kindness and humility, we'll never forget. Ordinary people who recognised suffering whether it had a name or not.